D1053011

Magic Pickle

AND THE PLANET OF THE GRAPES

BY SCOTT MORSE

A  Chapter Book

AN IMPRINT OF

■SCHOLASTIC

NEW YORK   TORONTO   LONDON   AUCKLAND   SYDNEY   MEXICO CITY   NEW DELHI   HONG KONG   BUENOS AIRES

For information regarding permission, write to
Scholastic Inc., Attention: Permissions Department,
557 Broadway, New York, NY 10012.

Library of Congress Cataloging-in-Publication Data

Morse, Scott.
Magic Pickle and the planet of the grapes : a Graphix illustrated
chapter book / by Scott Morse.
p. cm.
1. Comic books, strips, etc. I. Title.
PN6727.M678M34 2008
741.5--dc22

2007020539

41025981   4/09

ISBN-13: 978-0-439-87996-5
ISBN-10: 0-439-87996-5

10 9 8 7 6 5 4 3 2 1   08 09 10

First edition, March 2008
Printed in the U.S.A. 23

Edited by Sheila Keenan
Creative Director: David Saylor
Book Design by Charles Kreloff

Prologue

(or everything you need to know before you read this book)

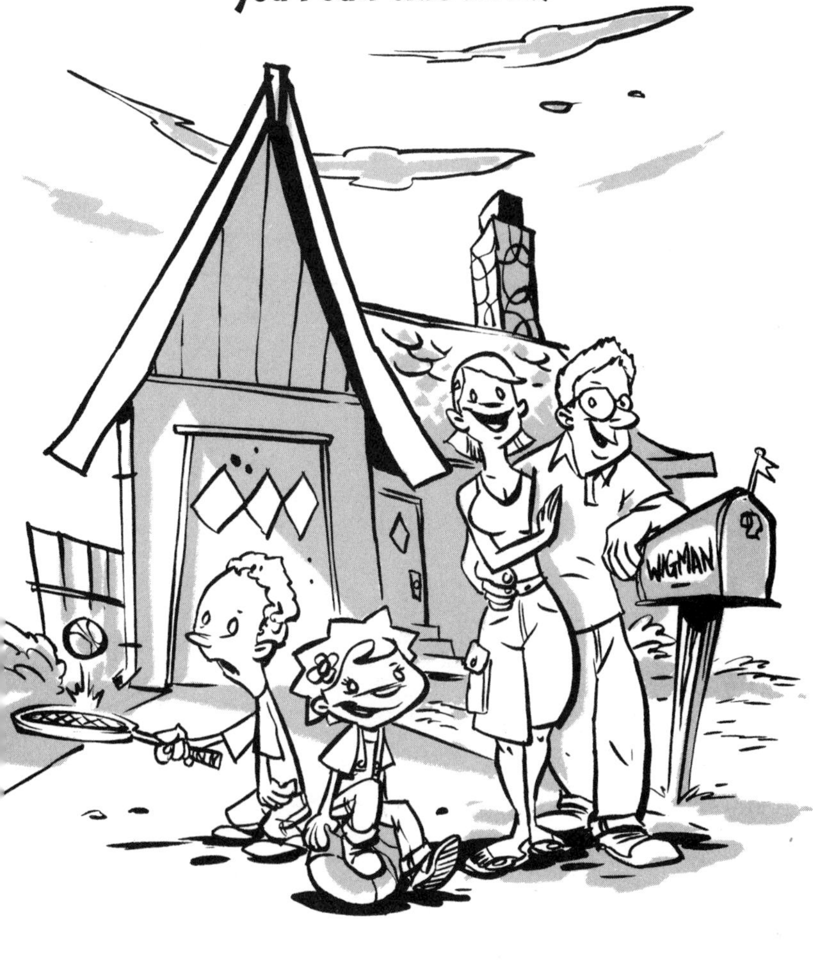
WIGMAN

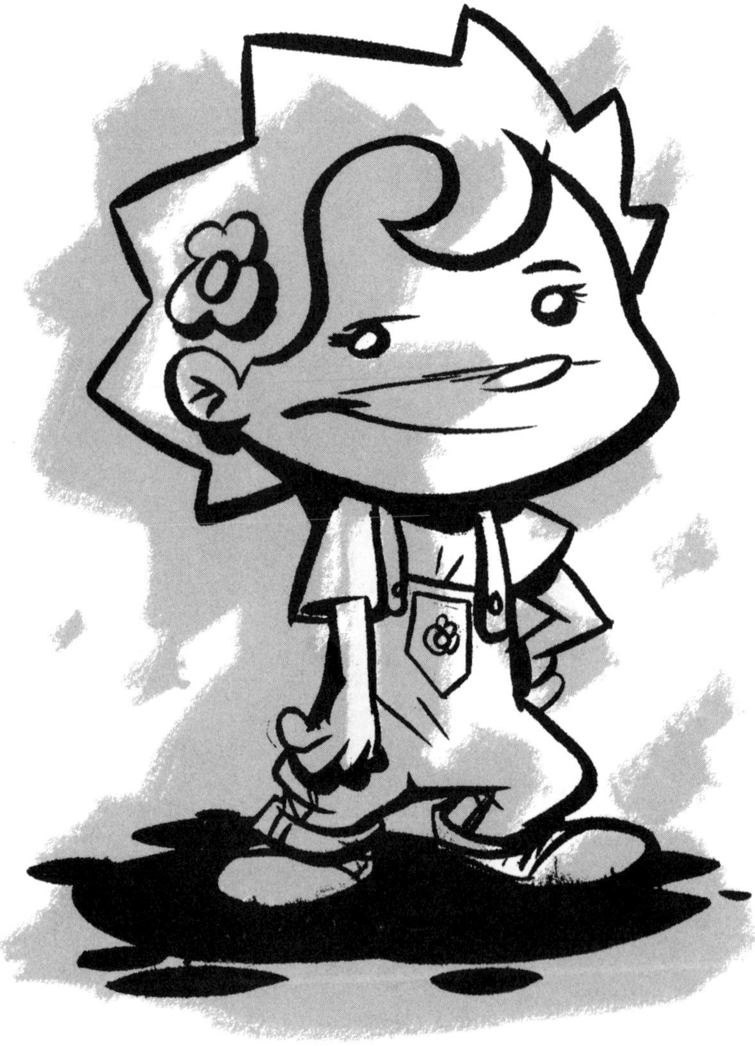

o Jo was pretty much like any kid next door. She lived with her dad, who was a top banana at Top Banana Computers; her mom, who was nuttier than peanut brittle, but a lot sweeter; and her brother, Jason, who was just goofy. The Wigmans' house was just like all the others on their block. Jo Jo even had her own bedroom on the first floor.

Or at least she'd thought it was her own.

One night, just as Jo Jo was about to fall asleep, something woke her up. Not just something . . . a huge **BANG!** And a **CRASH**.

Something had blasted a hole through her bedroom floor. Something that was stubby, green and bumpy. Something that could fly. Something that looked just like . . .

A pickle!

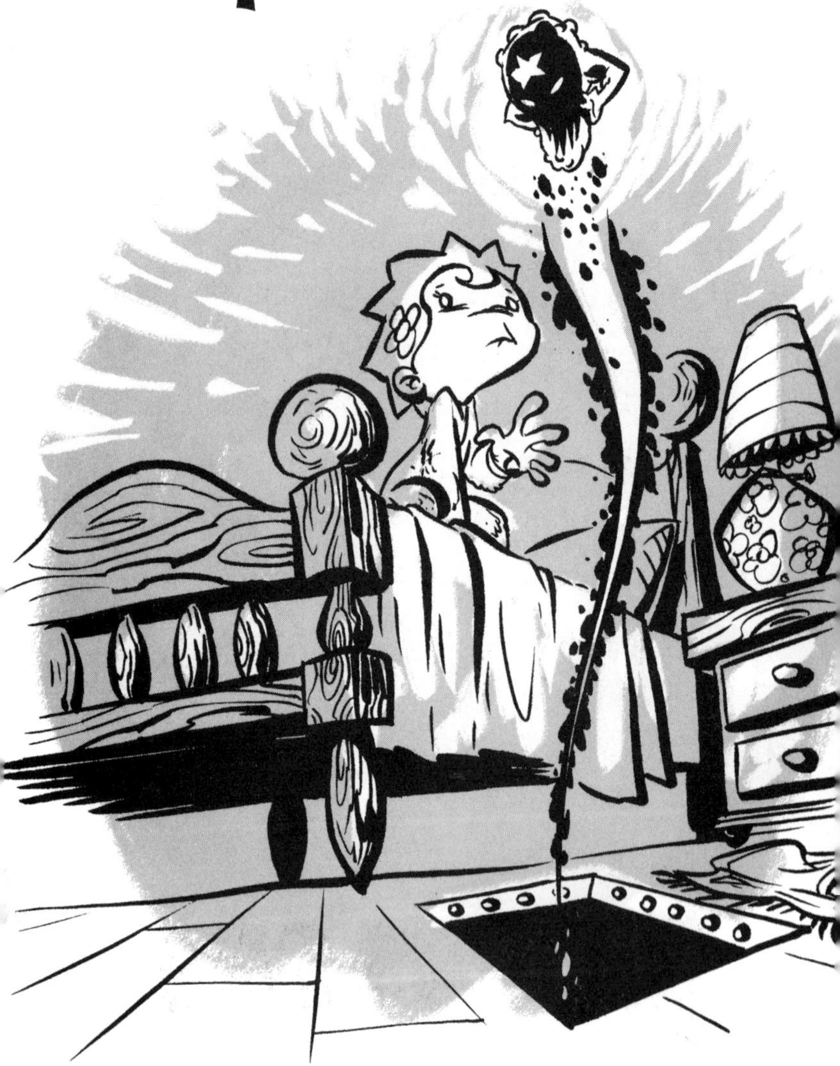

This pickle could talk, too. He used big words, the kind you usually have to look up in a dictionary. He kept talking about things like justice, and fighting crime, and saving the world from evil foods.

Jo Jo thought this pickle was nuts.

Turns out the Wigmans' house was accidentally built on top of Capital Dill, the secret underground lab of a secret government scientist named Dr. Jekyll Formaldehyde.

It was Dr. Formaldehyde's job to create a superhero to help protect the world. He *did* create the perfect hero, but it was kind of an accident. One day, when Dr. F. was eating lunch at his lab table (always a bad idea), his big, juicy kosher dill rolled in front of a gamma ray particle confabulator.

BOOM!

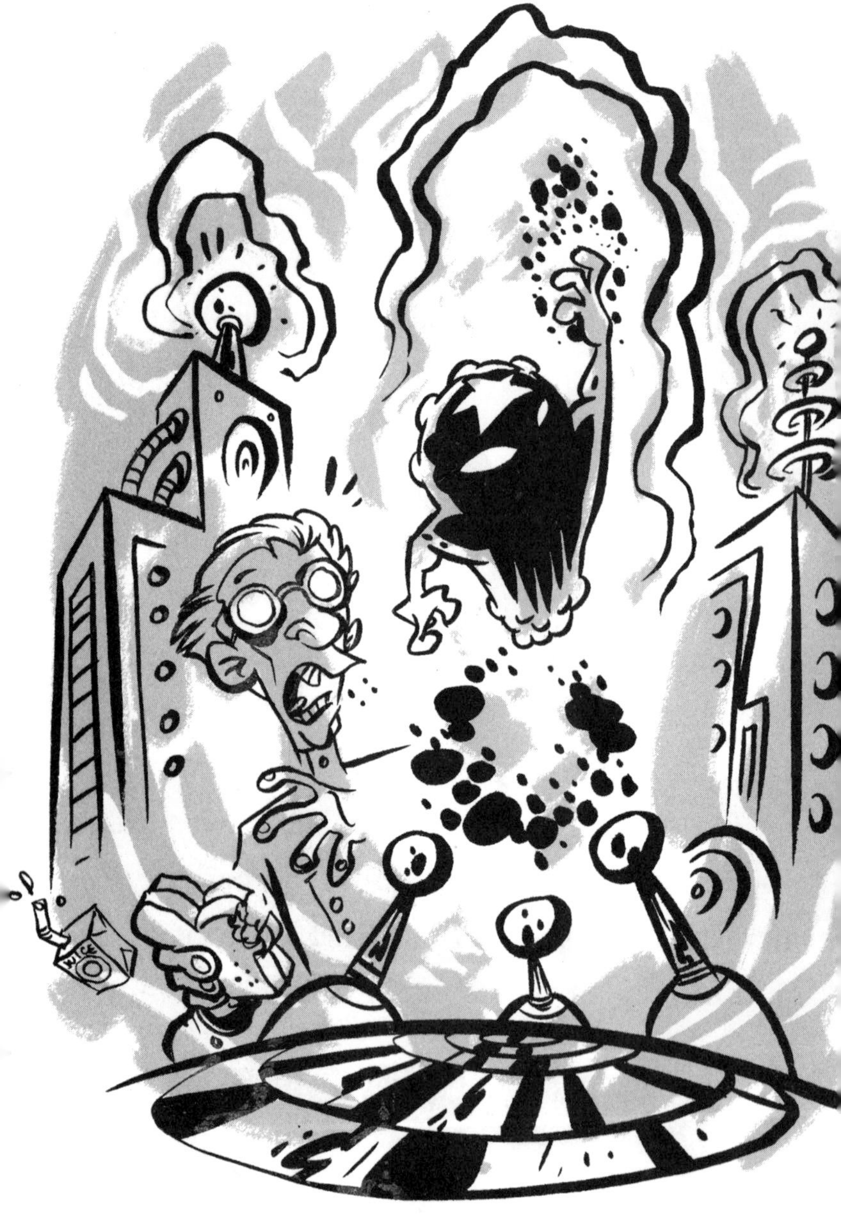

Out came a bumpy, green warrior with a blue star glowing on his forehead. Heroes always have some kind of cool costume in comic books. *This* pickle came with one of America's *symbols of truth and justice* stamped right on his noggin. He was pumping his powerful fists, ready to dish out dill justice.

Eureka! The superhero of Dr. Formaldehyde's dream. Okay, he *was* a pickle, with a really sour look in his eye, but he seemed to have really sweet powers. Dr. F. quickly realized this hero would stop at nothing to protect the world from all sorts of bad guys.

He decided to make a whole army and tossed the rest of his vegetarian combo lunch and fruit cup into the confabulator.

Not a very healthy idea. Total backfire! The food turned bad . . . *really* bad. Like, *EVIL* bad. The lettuce in his sandwich began to wrap around the doc's arm like some kind of lettuce-wrappy boa constrictor! A carrot attacked Dr. F.'s pet rabbit, then disappeared like a ghost. The peas shot around the room like crazy. Dr. Formaldehyde tried everything, but no amount of gooey dressing could swamp this insane salad. All the bad foods escaped into the night.

Dr. Formaldehyde's dream became a nightmare. He had mistakenly created **THE BROTHERHOOD OF EViL PRODUCE!** And these wicked fruits and veggies had one goal: to take over the world and bring forth the Salad Days, a new age where fruits and vegetables would reign supreme, and people would have to find some other food group to balance their diets.

The Brotherhood of Evil Produce kept growing and there was only one thing that could stop them: Dr. F.'s first creation, his kosher dill secret weapon.

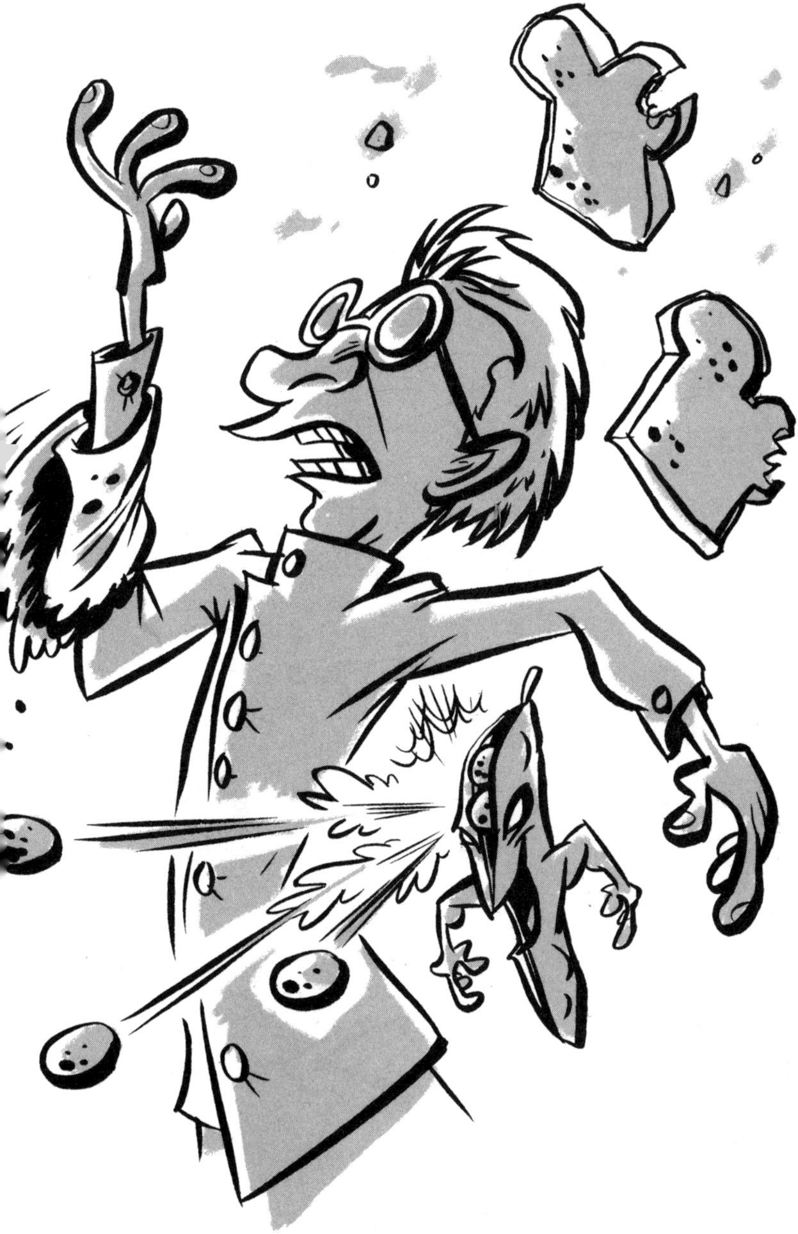

Dr. Formaldehyde launched himself into space in a special satellite. He circled the earth tracking the no-good food group and sending news of their tasteless plans back down to his kosher dill cohort in Capital Dill. It was up to Dr. F.'s super-pickle to save the world – from under little Jo Jo's bedroom floor.

And that's how Jo Jo came to share her room with a hush-hush, top-secret, flying Weapon Kosher superhero.

She liked to call him the Magic Pickle; it rolled off the tongue better.

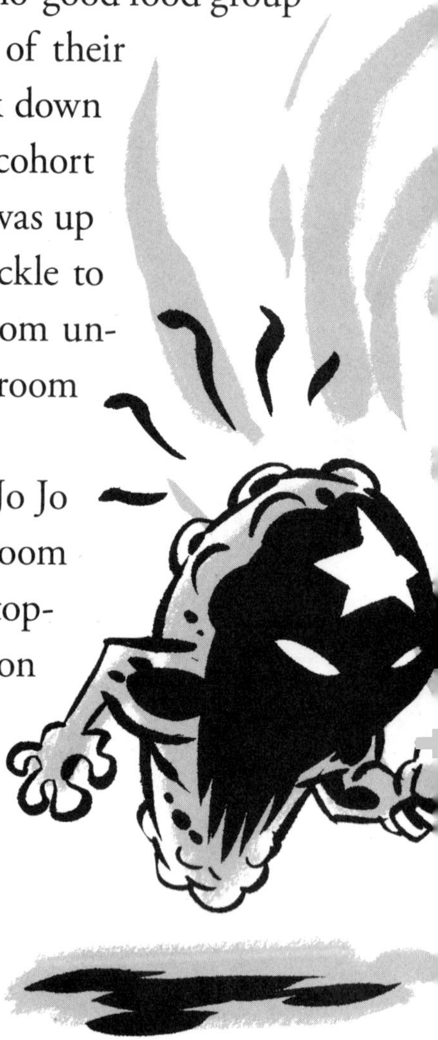

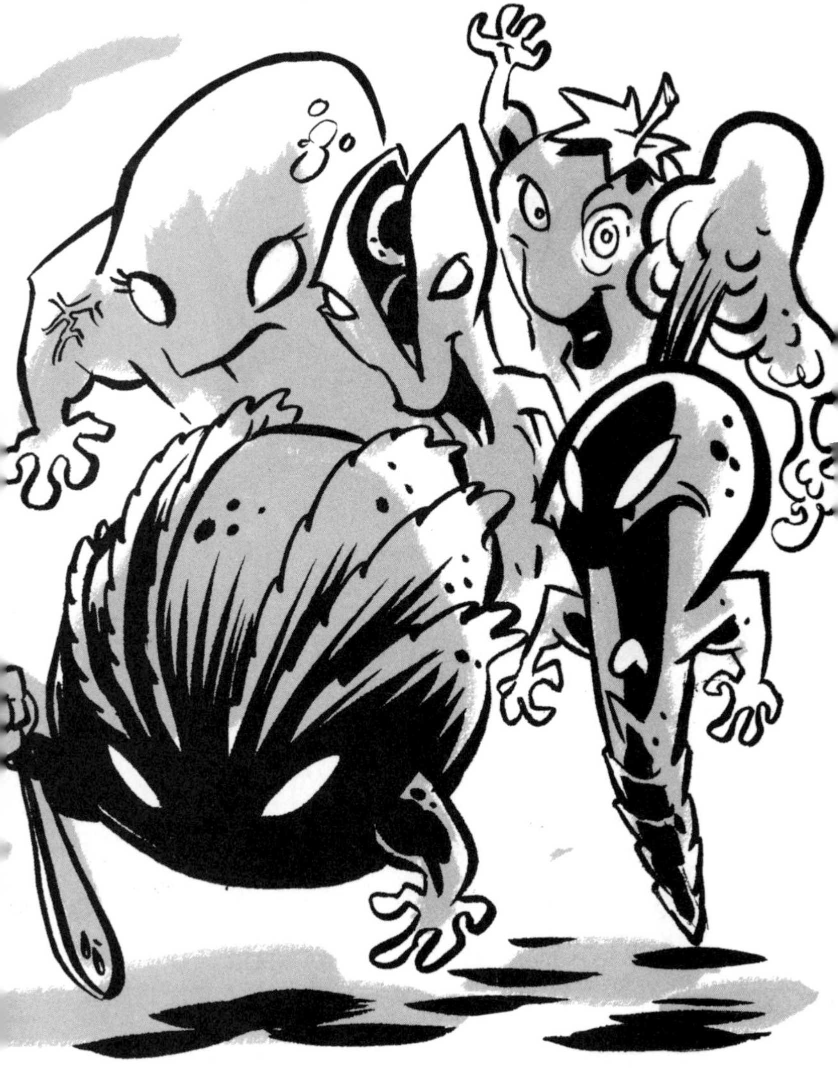

Chapter 1

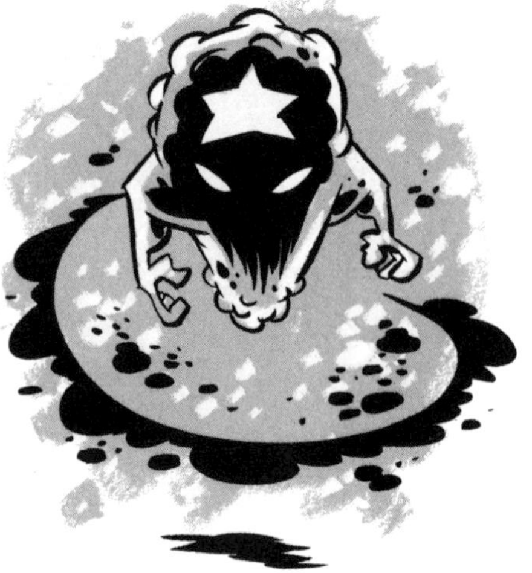

Bzzzzzzzzzzzzzzzz!!!

Something buzzed loudly in Jo Jo's ears. She pulled her pillow over her head.

Bzzzzzzzzzzzzzzzz!!!

She swatted the alarm clock. Slap! Slap!

"Five more minutes!" she mumbled into her pillow.

BLEEP! BLEEP! BLEEP!

Jo Jo tossed and turned until she was totally tangled up in her covers.

BLEEP!

Now she was wide awake. Something wasn't right. Today was Sunday. There was NO WAY she had set her alarm clock.

Jo Jo sat up in bed.

BOONG!

There was only one thing in the world that made that kind of sound: a computer, a giant, humongous, *Crime* Computer.

Like the one underneath her bed.

That briny, bumpy, green-bottom, slimy-noggin pickle!

Jo Jo jumped out of bed, frowning and rubbing her eyes.

"This is *way* too early!" she said. "Doesn't that dill-brain know how Sundays work?" She pushed aside the rug near her bed, threw open a secret hatch in the floorboards and stared down into a huge chamber filled with clunky metal machines. Tubes pumped green gas into boxes topped with blinking lightbulbs. Photos of funny-looking fruits and vegetables flashed across every computer screen. In the middle of all this whizzing and whirring floated an intense pickle whose muscles bulged like tight-stretched water

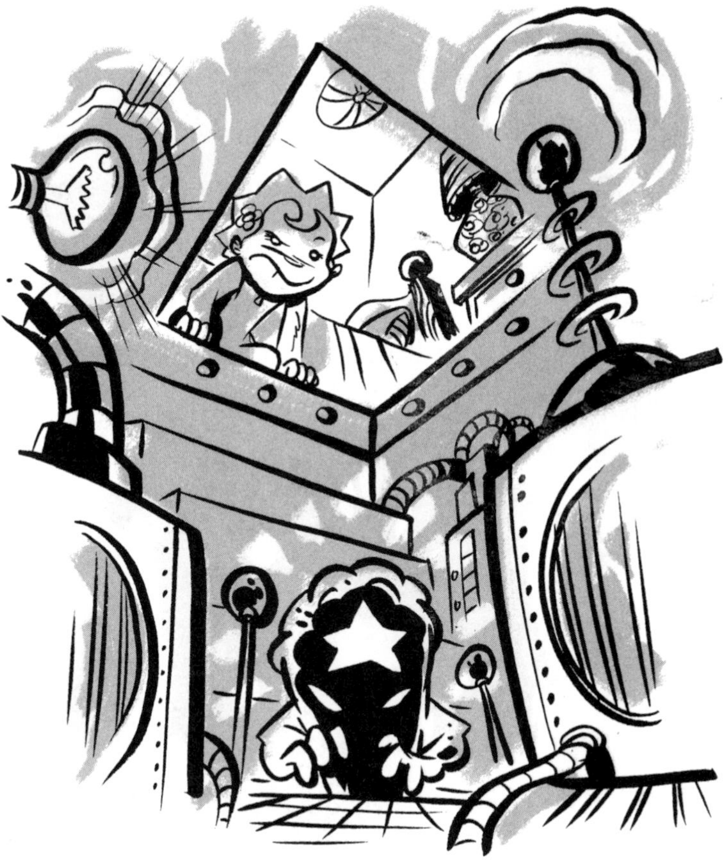

balloons and whose green fingers clicked away at the keyboard.

"You're kidding, right?" Jo Jo grumbled as she rubbed her eyes with her fists. "Didn't your Crime Computer come with a volume control? Or headphones?"

"Jo Jo! Good morning! Rise and shine!" answered the Magic Pickle.

"I'm using some new hardware to track some suspicious activity! It detects and analyzes mobile food energies like this sinister citrus. You'd be enhancing your education if you joined me promptly," he continued.

"I do not need my education enhanced today," said Jo Jo. "Today is one of two, count 'em, two days when there is no school, no rush to the school bus, NO NEED TO GET UP EARLY! Did you miss school the day they explained how a calendar works?!"

"The garden I grew up in was seasonal, but I hardly see how that matters at the moment," the Magic Pickle answered. He continued to rub his bumpy brow, study his equipment and type rapidly on his keyboard. A map of Hicksville appeared, with little yellow blips moving along a downtown street. One large blinking yellow dot appeared in the center of the street. Jo Jo's eyes lit up.

"That's the Farmers' Market! I almost forgot!" Jo Jo hurried back up toward her bedroom. "I'm supposed to meet Ellen there! We're on the hunt for the perfect basket of strawberries! I've got to get going!"

"It's the citrus *I'm* hunting," said the Magic Pickle.

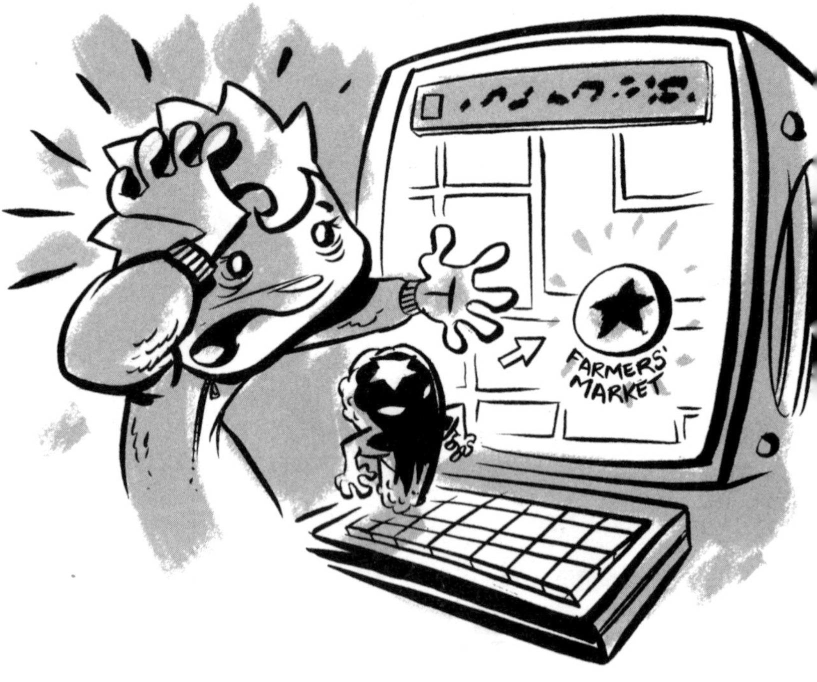
FARMERS'
MARKET

Chapter 2

Ellen Cranston lived just down the block from Jo Jo. Ellen had been Jo Jo's best friend since kindergarten, ever since she taught Jo Jo how to hide inside the little tunnel near the sandbox when the recess bell rang. Their teacher would actually growl like a dog while looking for them. The girls stayed hidden until their giggling gave them away.

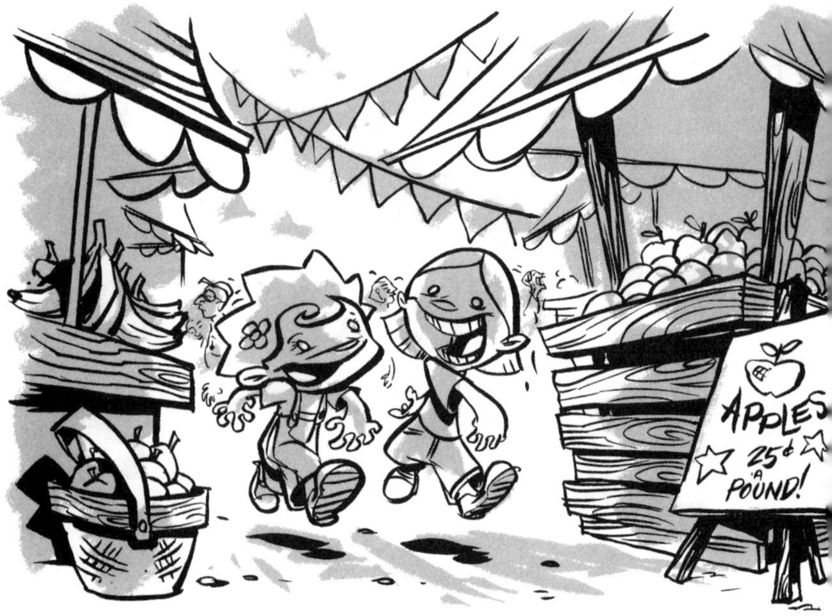
APPLES
25¢ A POUND!

Jo Jo found Ellen waiting on the corner of Main Street that, on Sundays, became the Farmers' Market. This was a large grouping of tents and tables, set up by local farms or orchards. Ellen grabbed Jo Jo's arm and dragged her into the maze of fruit and vegetable stands. They strolled past stalls stacked with tomatoes, broccoli, heads of lettuce and piles of watermelons.

"Did you bring the recipe?" Jo Jo asked Ellen.

Monday was the birthday of Binky Alawicious, their class hamster. Ellen thought they should bring in a cake, so her mom had copied down a strawberry shortcake recipe from her grandmother's cookbook.

"I've got it. This is gonna be so good!" Ellen exclaimed. She pulled out a piece of paper from her pocket. "I'm tellin' you, we're gonna be class heroes for baking the best cake in the world!"

WHHHSSSHHH!

Jo Jo's eyes fluttered. She thought she'd just seen a green flash in the air.

"Did you hear something?" Jo Jo asked Ellen. "Like a green light?"

"Did I *hear* a green *light*?" Ellen asked with a raised eyebrow. "I don't know . . . did you just *smell* me a dumb question?" She giggled and nudged Jo Jo in the shoulder. "Weirdo."

"Heh, heh, yeah, silly . . . " Jo Jo chuckled nervously.

Jo Jo had learned to look out for strange vegetables and fruits in the most unexpected places. The Magic Pickle had warned her that those bad seeds, the Brotherhood of Evil Produce, could strike at any time.

Jo Jo took another quick look around. It was probably nothing.

Ellen spotted a sign for a strawberry stand and she and Jo Jo raced toward it.

"I can practically taste the juice running down my chin from those yummy berries," Ellen drooled.

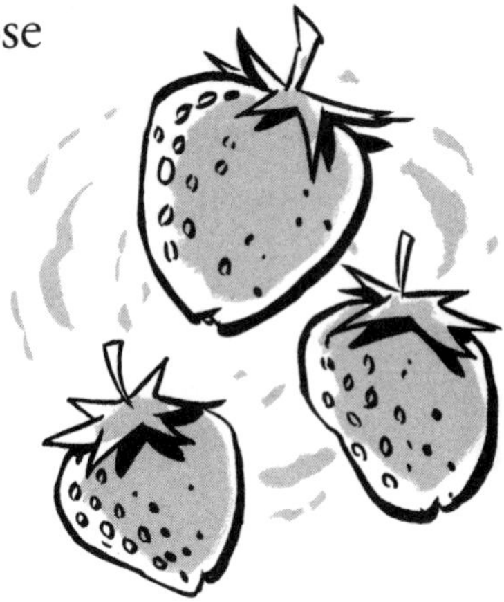

The girls rounded a corner and skidded to a stop in front of the strawberry stand.

Their jaws dropped.

Someone was buying the very last basket of beautiful, scrumptious strawberries. And that someone was a girl in their class: *Lu Lu Deederly!*

Lu Lu was taller than both Jo Jo and Ellen. She had curly hair and freckles, and almost always had a sneer on her face.

"I believe this is exact change, sir," Lu Lu said with her famous sneer. She handed the fruitseller a fistful of quarters.

"Perfect! Thanks," said the fruitseller.

"I'm known for being perfect," Lu Lu winked. She turned to Jo Jo and Ellen and sneered her perfect sneer one more time.

"Mmmm . . . these will taste *so* good in my lunch tomorrow," Lu Lu cooed. She plucked a strawberry from the basket and took a big, wet bite. "It's so great that I get to eat lunch *early*, too, since I'm the lunchroom helper this week." Strawberry juice streamed down

Lu Lu's chin. She really knew how to rub it in. Jo Jo was about to lose her cool any second. Ellen grabbed her arm to lead her away.

"Come on, Jo Jo, let's let Lu Lu stew in her juices. Maybe there's a lemonade stand nearby," Ellen said.

Lu Lu bit into another big, fat strawberry right in front of them.

"It's okay, Ellen. I'll share with you and Jo Jo," Lu Lu said. She batted her eyes. She didn't look very sincere. "Hold out your hands."

Lu Lu dropped the leafy stems of the strawberries she'd already eaten into their hands. There was still a small bit of fruit on each one, just enough to make their palms sticky.

"Now don't eat them all at once! You might get a tummy ache," Lu Lu snickered as she skipped away.

"How about we go find that lemonade now," Jo Jo said with a frown. "I really need to cool off."

"You aren't the only one," agreed Ellen.

Chapter 3

Jo Jo and Ellen turned another corner. A man stormed past them with a scowl on his face. He pushed past a woman with a baby.

HUFF!

Then he threw a paper cup at a nearby trash can. The paper cup bounced off the rim and onto the head of a dog. **BOP!**

The dog growled at the man.

ROWF!
ROWF!
ROWWFF!!

The man growled at the dog. "Oh, rowf, yourself!" he said, then disappeared down another aisle of the Farmers' Market.

"That litterbugging guy was even ruder than Lu Lu!" said Ellen. "Who would actually stop and bark at a dog?!"

"Maybe the lemonade made him a sourpuss," Jo Jo said. She pointed to a nearby table. "I think he got it over there. That table's got a cup on it like the one he threw."

"Whatever, I'm thirsty," said Ellen. "Let's get some and hope it doesn't pucker our brains too much." The girls walked up to the table.

"Hey, who do we pay? HELLO?" Ellen called.

"Look," Jo Jo said. She pointed to a sign propped against a small pyramid of lemons:

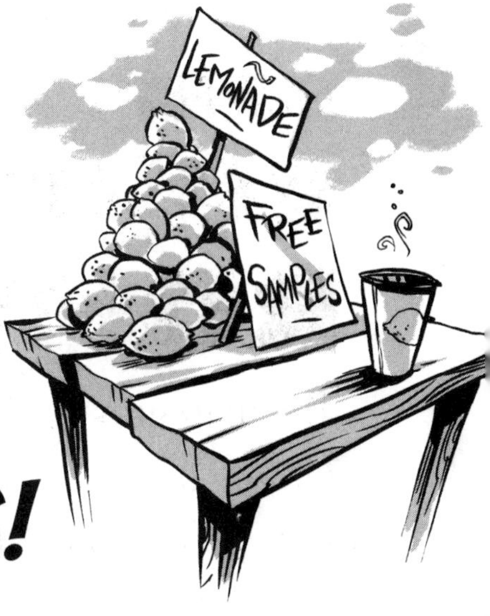
LEMONADE
FREE SAMPLES

FREE SAMPLES!

There was one cup of lemonade left.

"Wanna flip a coin to see who gets it?" Ellen asked Jo Jo.

"I guess," Jo Jo said. "I'd share it, but I really don't want your cooties."

"HA-HA, very funny." Ellen reached in her pocket for a quarter.

Suddenly, a wild-haired boy pushed in between Jo Jo and Ellen.

"Hey, watch it, lemonhead! There's a line!" Ellen blurted.

"Isn't that Jarek from our class?" asked Jo Jo.

The boy grabbed the last cup of lemonade and gulped it down right in front of them. He finished the whole cup in one swallow.

GLU-GUULLPP!

"Hey, buddy, come up for air!" Jo Jo teased.

"I'm sorry, I was just so thirsty and—" Jarek suddenly stopped speaking. His eyes

narrowed. A huge frown formed on his
forehead.

"What are you lookin' at?" he demanded.

Jo Jo and Ellen didn't know what to say.
This kid was suddenly as rude as everyone
else they'd seen today!

WHOOOSH!

A sudden wind blew Ellen's hair into her face.

"OH, come ON!" Ellen cried. "Now the wind is against us, too!"

PPPLLTT! PPPPLLLLTTTTT!

"Binky Alawicious better appreciate all the trouble we're going through!" she said, spitting hair out of her mouth.

"What—?" Jo Jo muttered. Was that something green flying past?

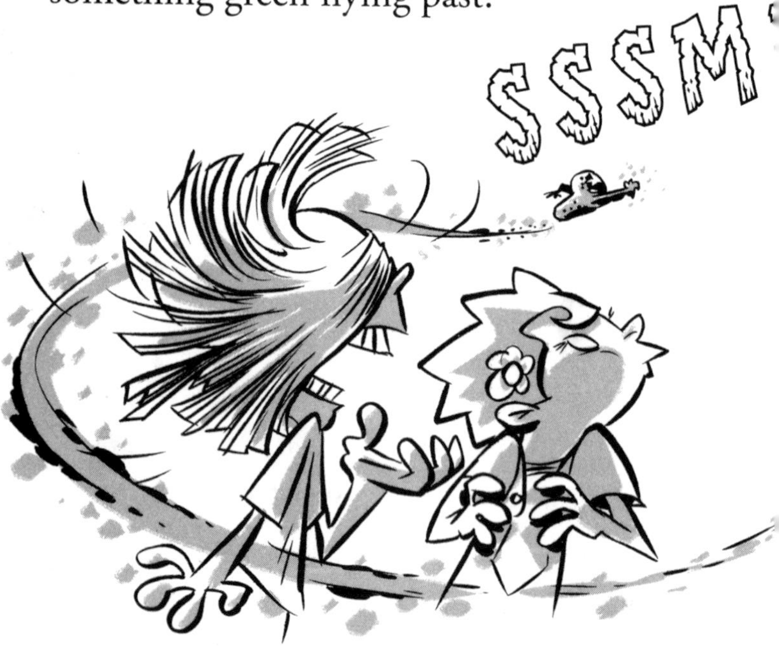
SSSM

AAASHHH!

The lemonade table flipped over. Jo Jo saw a streak of green energy whiz down a back alley. No one else noticed; they were too busy watching the lemon pyramid topple. Lemons rolled down the street, every which way. Shoppers glared at Jo Jo, Ellen and Jarek, since they were closest to the table.

"Quit starin' at me! Mind yer own business!" Jarek snapped at the other shoppers.

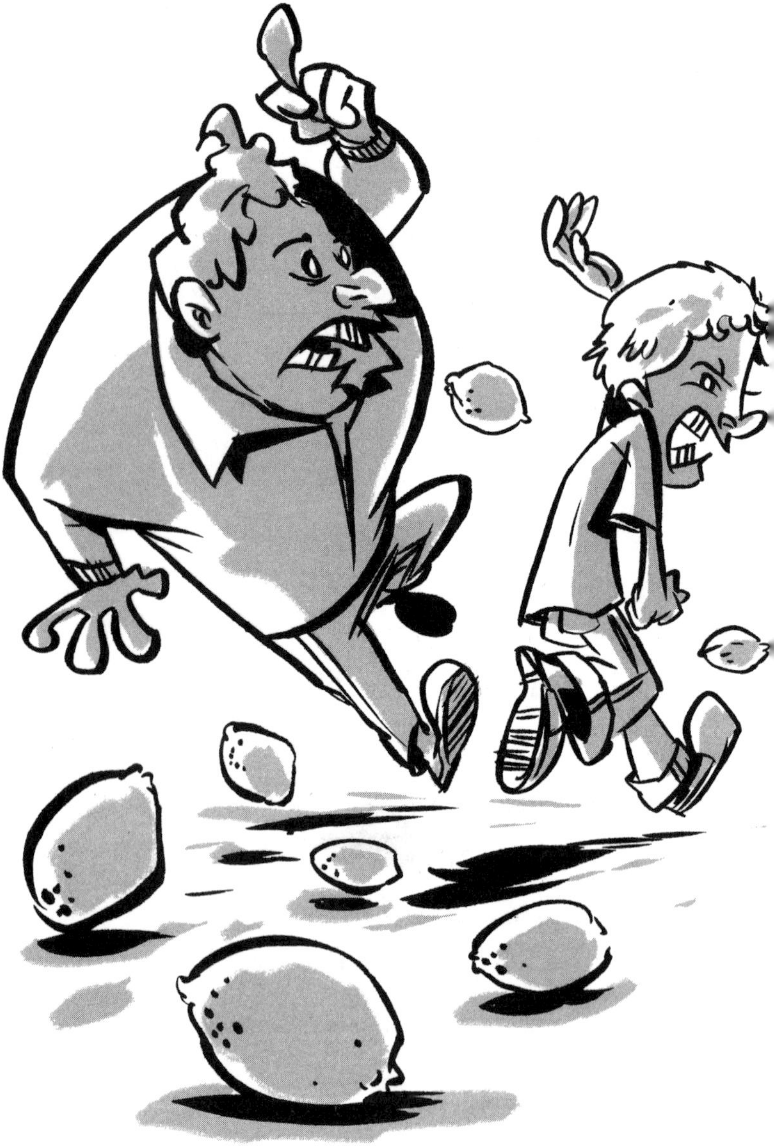

Jarek's acting differently than he normally does at school, Jo Jo thought. Jarek was usually kind of shy and quiet—definitely not rude.

"I can't see a thing!" Ellen complained. She was still trying to get her hair out of her eyes. This was going to take time. Ellen had a lot of hair.

Jarek kicked away the lemons that wobbled at his feet.

"You better pick those up, young man!" a shopper insisted, wagging a finger at Jarek.

"Pick 'em up yourself, sucker!" Jarek snarled. "This ain't my mess! Yer all squeezin' me the wrong way! I'm outta here!" Jo Jo watched Jarek stomp off. Definitely not that same quiet kid from school.

"There! WHEW!" Ellen finally brushed the rest of her hair out from in front of her eyes.

WHOOOOSSSHHHH!

Another gust of wind blew. Ellen's hair flew right back in front of her face.

"Awww, man!"

Out of the corner of her eye, Jo Jo spotted a faint green streak again. It disappeared behind a big van in the parking lot.

"I've gotta go to the bathroom, Ellen. Wait here!" Jo Jo blurted as she ran off. The mess at the lemonade stand was no accident, and Jo Jo knew just who had caused it.

The Magic Pickle.

But why?

Chapter 4

Jo Jo stopped by a big van with an apple tree painted on its side. But there was something wrong with the picture.

"That green apple up there is too lumpy," said Jo Jo. "It looks like a sack full of peas!"

"And you look like a sack full of sarcasm," said the green apple.

"Don't be such a crabapple."

Jo Jo smiled. The strange-looking apple wasn't an apple at all. The Magic Pickle hovered away from the painting and toward Jo Jo, cautiously looking around.

"Shhh! I hope you've taken the proper precautions! My appearance in public could cause panic," said the Magic Pickle. "The people of the world, who I've sworn to protect under my umbrella of pickled chivalry, must never truly know that my existence isn't counterfeit!"

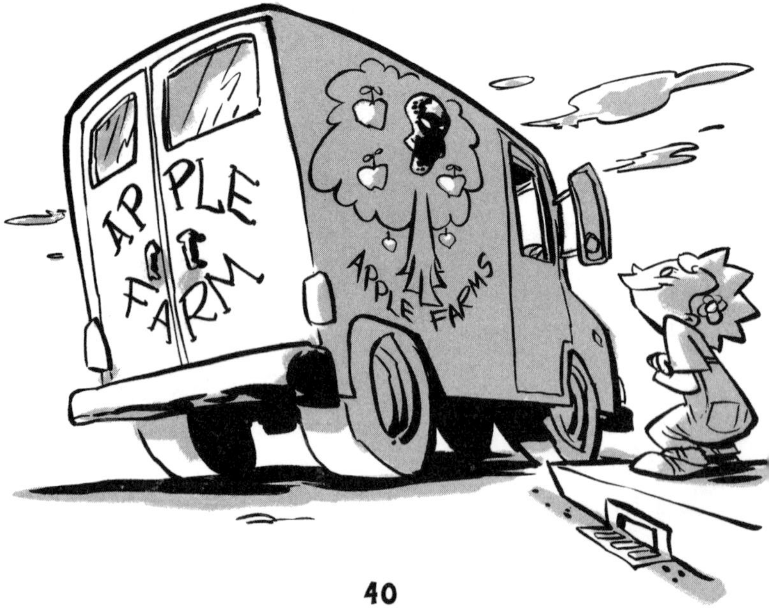
APPLE FARM
APPLE FARMS

Jo Jo stared at the Magic Pickle. She still wasn't used to all the big words he used. Every conversation was like a vocabulary quiz.

"Smaller words, bumpy," she said. "It's Sunday, remember? I try to give the dictionary part of my brain the weekends off."

"I need to stay hidden," the Magic Pickle replied simply. "Most people wouldn't understand that I'm an agent of justice."

"You would freak people out," agreed Jo Jo. "Or else make them hungry. So *why* did you blow up the lemonade stand?"

"Foul play was at hand. Or sour play, at least," answered the Magic Pickle. "Working overtime with my Crime Computer, I uncovered a series of clues that led me here to the Farmers' Market. It appears that my old enemies, the Brotherhood of Evil Produce, planned to unleash a sour potion on the public, disguised as lemonade. Anyone who drank it would behave in a foul manner."

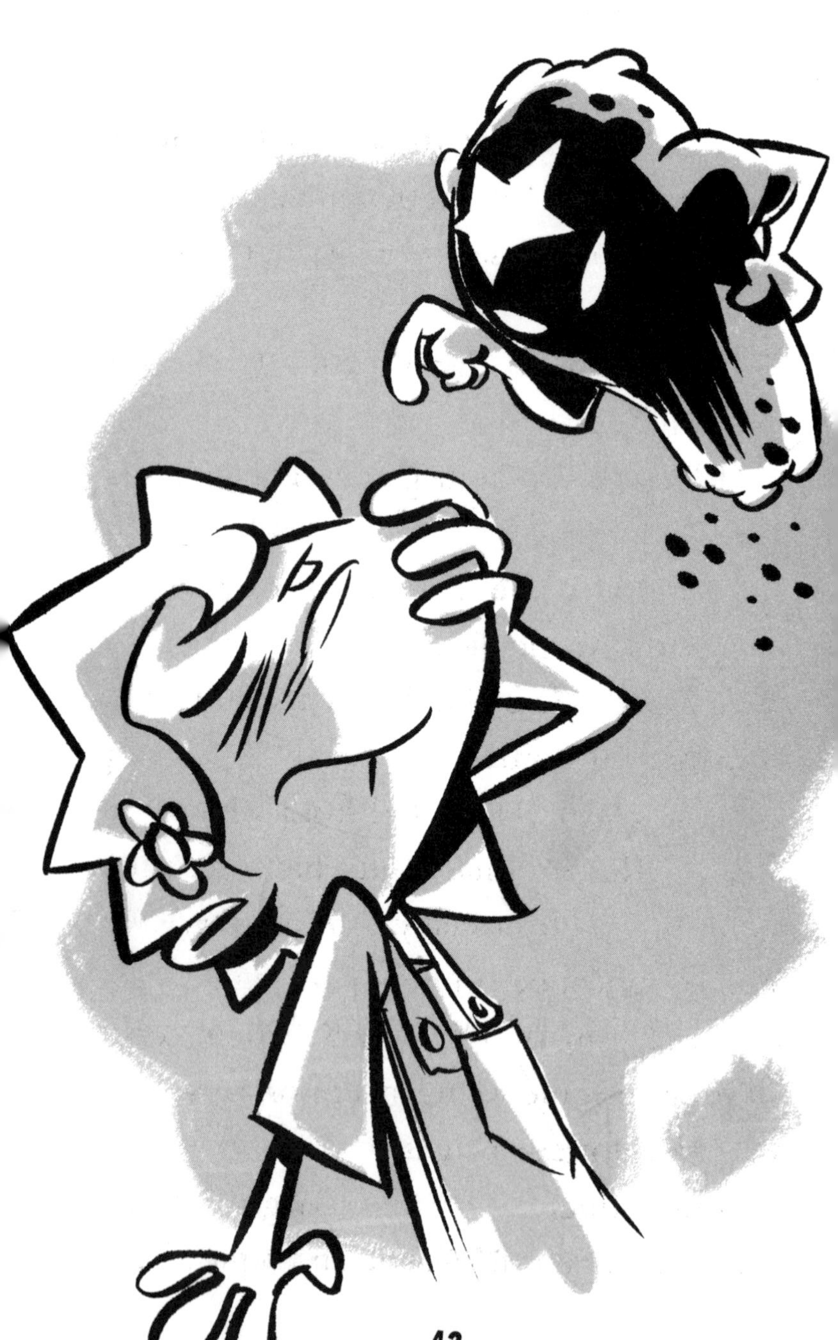

"So *that's* why all those people were so rude after they left the lemonade stand. A bunch of sourpusses, feeling sour grapes," said Jo Jo.

"There were no grapes involved," said the Magic Pickle.

"I know that. 'Sour grapes' is a figure of speech," Jo Jo said.

"Who was the boy at the lemonade stand?" the Magic Pickle asked, getting back to business. "He had quite an assortment of ill-mannered words."

"That's Jarek. He's a kid from school," Jo Jo said. "That lemonade must have puckered up his brain. He's usually sort of quiet." She tried to remember more about Jarek. "He's also really smart. He actually volunteered to bring in some weird invention to school tomorrow for extra credit."

"Interesting," said the Magic Pickle. "Keep an eye on this 'Jarek' and report back

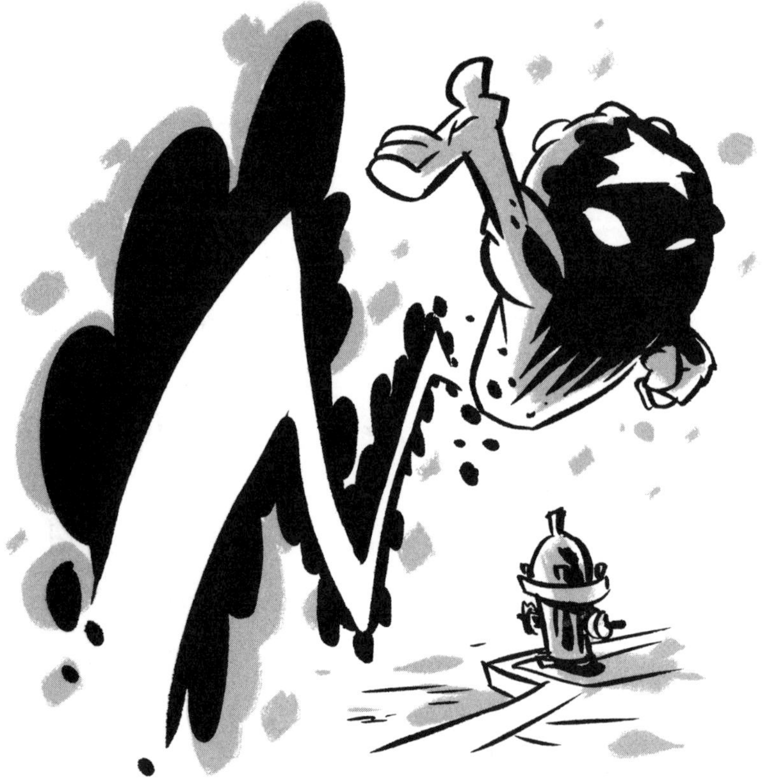

to me if you notice any suspicious activity. He's infected with the sourness of the lemonade, and there's no telling how long it might last."

Jo Jo saluted the Magic Pickle.

"Good luck with your lemon war. Find that lemonade culprit! Fight the sour, man," she said with a smile.

"Indeed," said the Magic Pickle. He flew off down the street in a blurry burst of green.

Jo Jo worked her way back to the lemonade stand. Ellen had pulled her hair back into a ponytail so that it stayed out of her face.

"I'm not taking any more chances with this wind," she said.

"I think the storm's blown through," said Jo Jo.

"Whatever. At least I figured out how we can still make strawberry shortcake,"

said Ellen. "We just need a couple of jars of strawberry jam! That'll work, right?"

Jo Jo shrugged. "At the very least we can throw in some peanut butter and call it lunch."

Suddenly, Jarek appeared, pulling a red wagon.

"Outta the way, outta the way," said Jarek as he elbowed past the girls.

Jarek stopped at a nearby booth. He had a weird look in his eyes. He handed the fruitseller there a wad of money.

"Here ya go, buddy. I want to fill 'er up," Jarek said.

"Err, uh . . . fill what up?" the fruitseller asked.

Jarek gestured to his wagon.

"I want every grape you got."

The fruitseller looked at the wad of money, then shoved it in his apron pocket.

"Money talks, kid, and yours just told me

you really like grapes," said the fruitseller.

"Well, good thing we're not making grape shortcake." Ellen sighed. "Jarek just cleaned that guy out!"

"Let's get outta here," Jo Jo said. "This is the weirdest Sunday I've had all month."

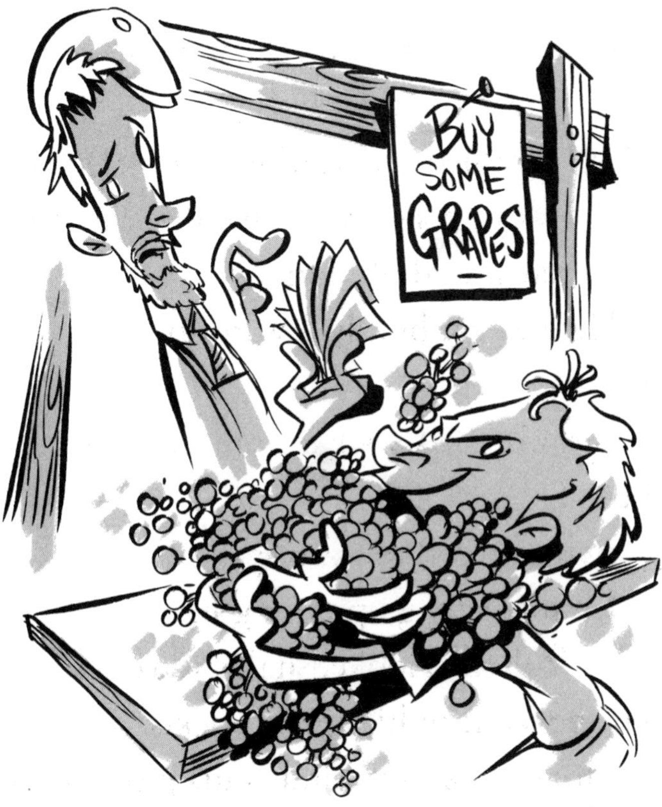
BUY
SOME
GRAPES

Chapter 5

Jo Jo's mom kissed her good night and turned off the bedroom light; luckily she didn't notice the faint glow of computer lights coming from under the floorboards. As soon as her mother closed the door, Jo Jo hopped out of bed. She flipped aside the throw rug, pulled open the secret entrance to Capital Dill and climbed on down.

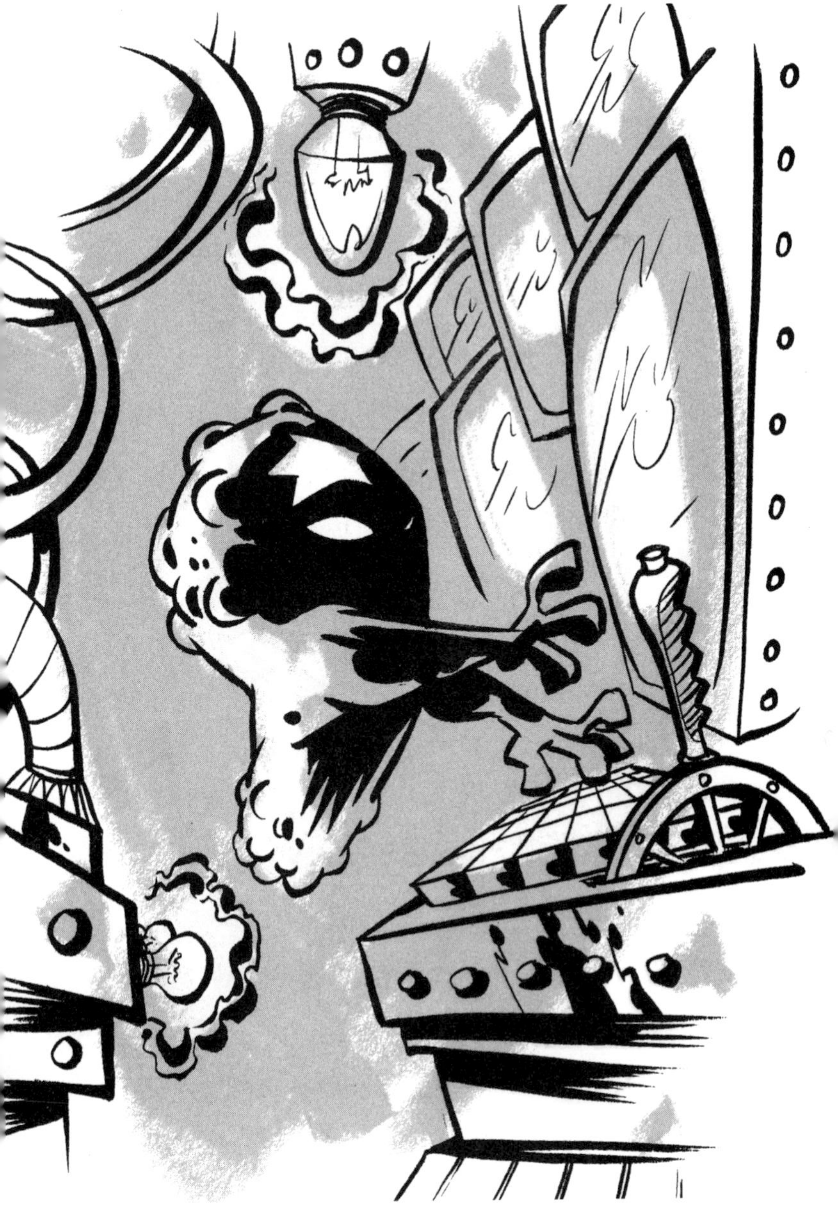

The Magic Pickle was busy on his computer. He hovered as he typed. He always hovered.

"You'd probably roll over like an egg if you tried to sit down," Jo Jo giggled.

"If I didn't know any better, I'd suspect you were in league with The One-Limer and Orange Quip," said the Magic Pickle. "Their jokes are about as clever as yours."

"Are they locked up with the rest of your weirdo bad-guys?" Jo Jo asked. She glanced down the hallway of Capital Dill that led to the refrigerated cell block where the Magic Pickle locked up all of his vegetable enemies. He called it his Frozen Food Section.

"It's like walking past a vending machine down there," Jo Jo said with a shiver.

"Joke if you must," the Magic Pickle warned, "but rest peacefully at night knowing that the world is safe from these incredible inedibles."

The Magic Pickle's computer screen flashed a grid of mug shots; most had a red X across them.

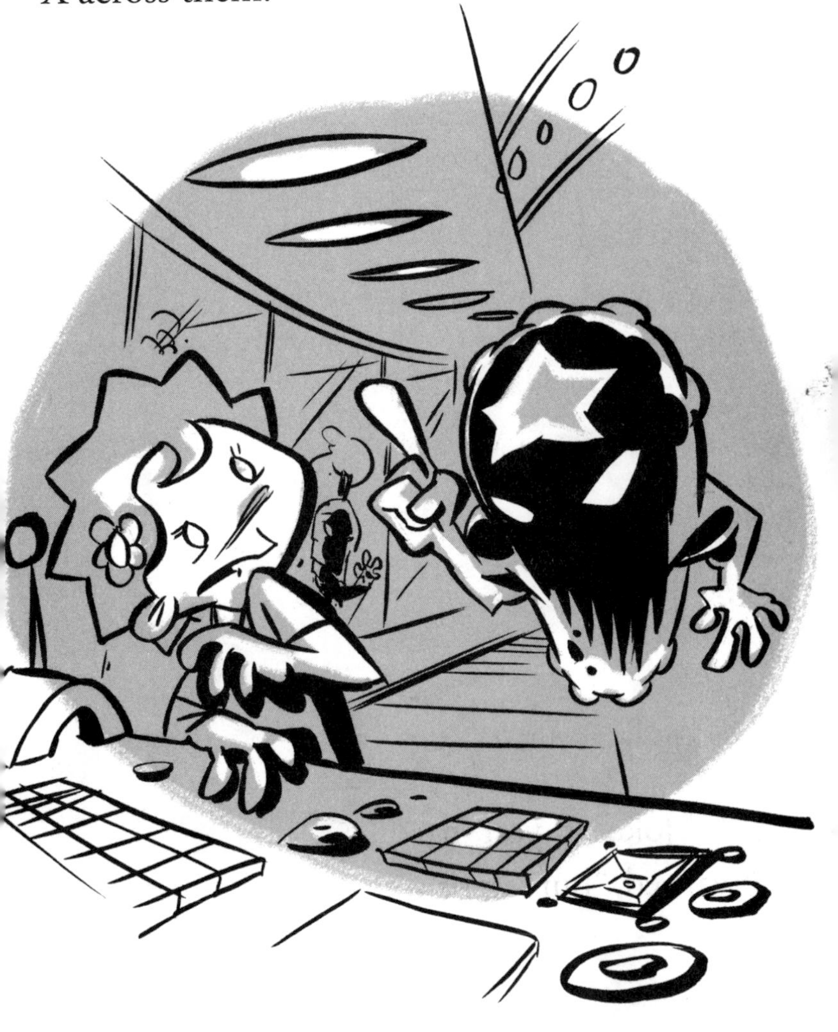

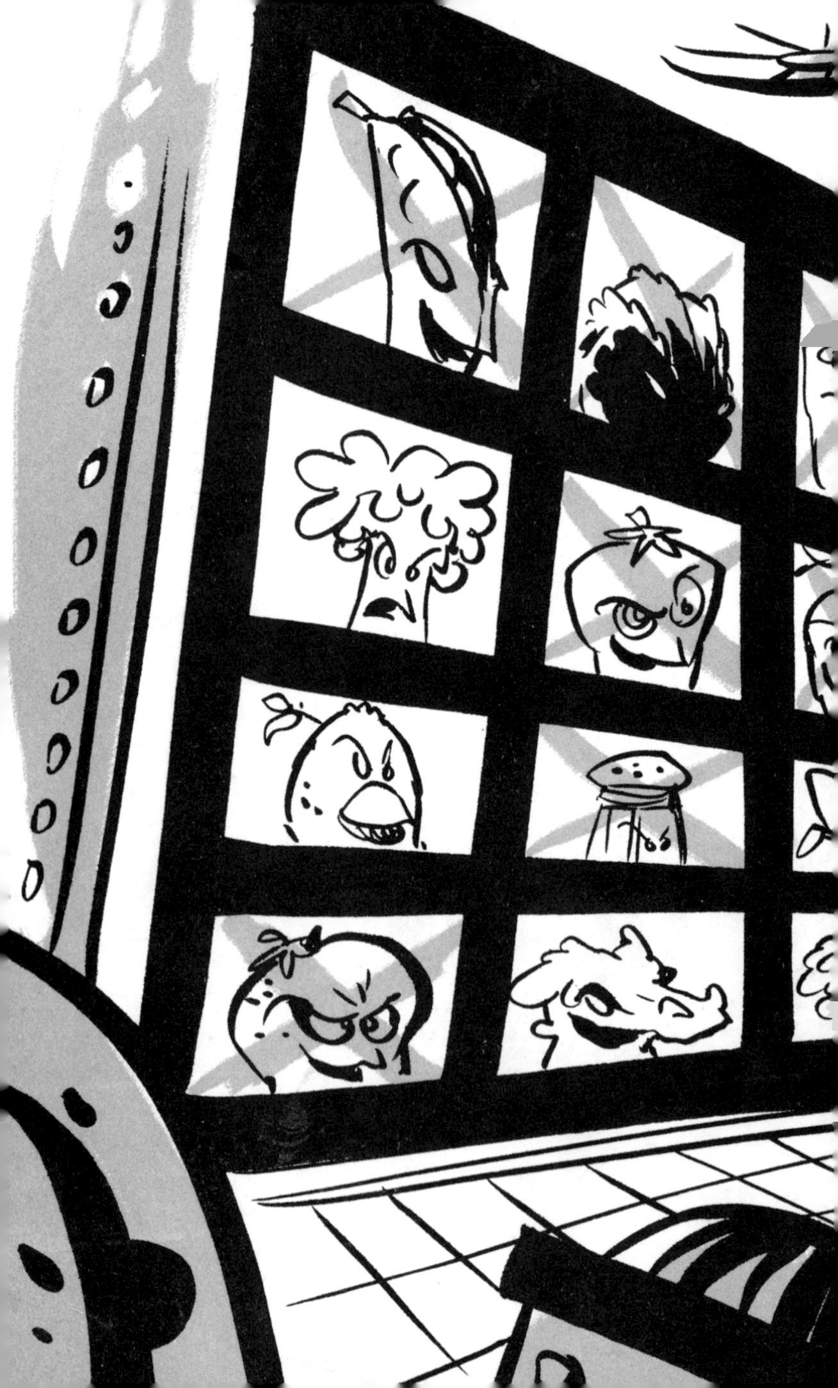

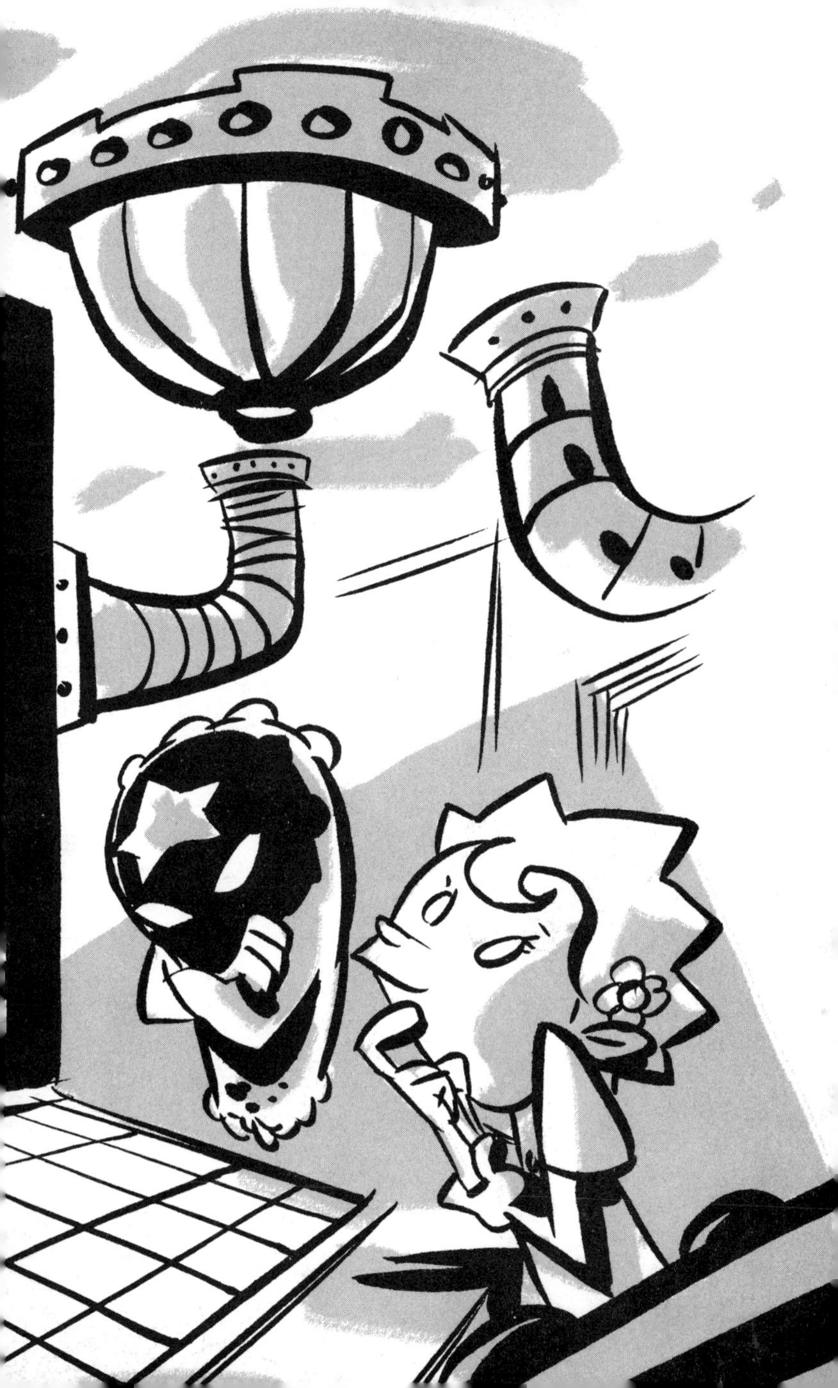

"Rotten, each and every one of them. Well past their pull dates," the Magic Pickle said. "You see? **ROMAINE GLADIATOR**: apprehended. **THE PHANTOM CARROT**: apprehended. **PEA SHOOTER**: apprehended. All on ice," the Magic Pickle assured Jo Jo.

But a few of the veggie villains weren't covered by red Xs.

"What about those guys?" Jo Jo asked.

"I'm afraid they're still at large, hiding or making mischief," the Magic Pickle answered. "But they'll make an interesting salad when I catch them all."

"Well, before you start shaking up the ranch dressing, I just remembered something. We saw Jarek again before we left the Farmers' Market," Jo Jo offered, changing the subject.

The Magic Pickle spun around.

"Did you observe him in the act of anything strange?" he asked.

"If you call buying a whole wagonload of grapes *strange*, then yep," Jo Jo answered.

"Interesting. Interesting indeed," said the Magic Pickle. "Did the look of sourness from the lemonade remain in the young man's eyes?"

"Jarek wasn't acting *sweet*, I'll tell you that much," said Jo Jo. "I'm starting to think maybe he's a kind of mad scientist. He's supposed to bring in some sort of invention for extra credit tomorrow."

The Magic Pickle spun back around and tapped a few buttons on his keyboard. He watched as the computer screen scrolled through more pictures of bad guys.

"Hmmm. It doesn't seem poetic enough for The Rhyming Lime to be involved," he said. "I don't think Honeydo and Honeydon't would be able to agree on a plan. And it just sounds way too crazy to be Hazel the Nut."

"What are you talking about?" asked Jo Jo, confused.

"Jarek. Grapes. I've never crossed paths with any grape-related agents of evil, I'm afraid. I'd better study up in case we're faced with some new kind of threat," the Magic Pickle admitted. "I just can't figure out why anyone would purchase so many grapes. The Brotherhood must somehow be involved . . . but how?"

"Look, I gotta get back to bed. It *is* a school night," Jo Jo reminded the Magic Pickle.

"I'll keep an eye on Jarek tomorrow."

"I recommend you keep *both* eyes on him," the Magic Pickle suggested.

Jo Jo rolled *both* eyes and went up to bed.

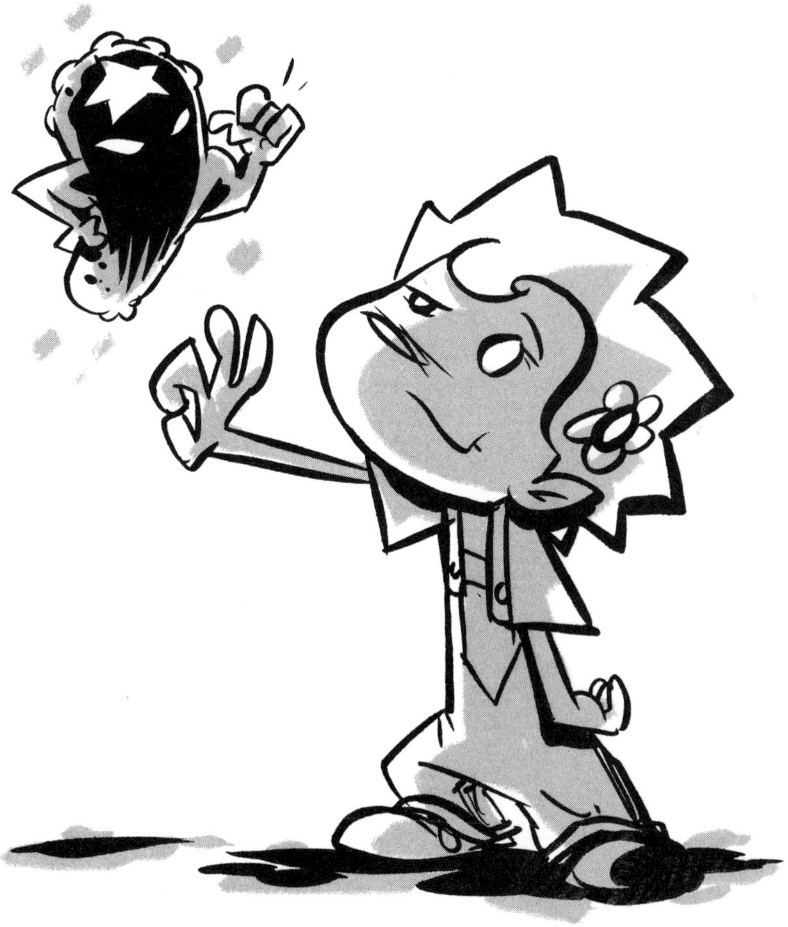

Chapter 6

"Jarek looks like a zombie!" Ellen whispered to Jo Jo.

"He looks like he didn't get any sleep, that's for sure," Jo Jo agreed.

The girls watched Jarek walk up to the front of the class. He stood next to something big and bulgy; it was covered by a bedsheet. A thick cord hung out from beneath the

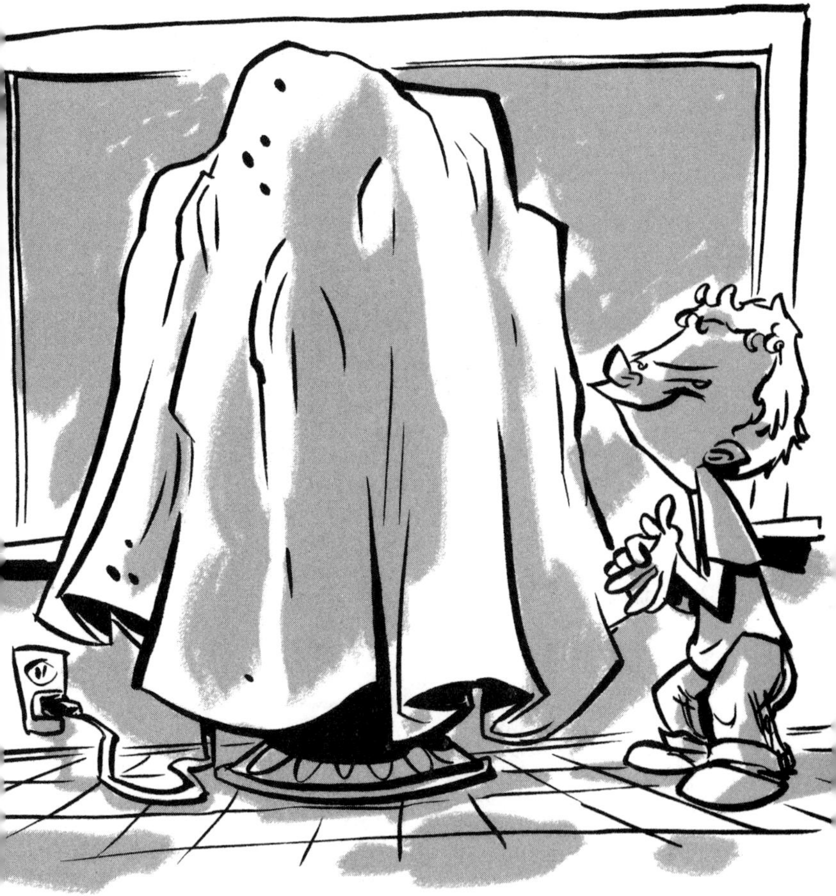

sheet; it was plugged into a socket.

Jarek's invention.

Jo Jo, Ellen and the rest of the class watched eagerly.

"You think it's a time machine?" Mikey Spuchins whispered to Jo Jo. "I bet it's a time machine. I bet you he's from the future."

Mikey lived across the street from Jo Jo. He was full of big ideas.

"Jarek's been in our class since kindergarten," Jo Jo whispered back. "I think we'd know by now if he was from the future."

"You're right," said Mikey. "That makes him from the *past*, since we knew him way back then. Duh."

Jo Jo groaned. Their teacher, Miss Emilyek, cleared her throat.

"You might all remember that Jarek promised us something special for today," announced Miss Emilyek.

Mikey leaned close to Jo Jo's ear again.

"Maybe Jarek can take us into the future, and we can skip right into next summer," Mikey said. "Or at least maybe we can skip math this afternoon."

"Maybe it's some sort of anti-language machine that'll help you to stop talking," Jo Jo answered. Mikey stuck his tongue out at her.

Miss Emilyek turned to Jarek.

"Jarek, would you like to show us your experiment?" Miss Emilyek asked sweetly. Jarek's eyes darted quickly from the students to Miss Emilyek to the mystery object. Then he whipped the sheet off.

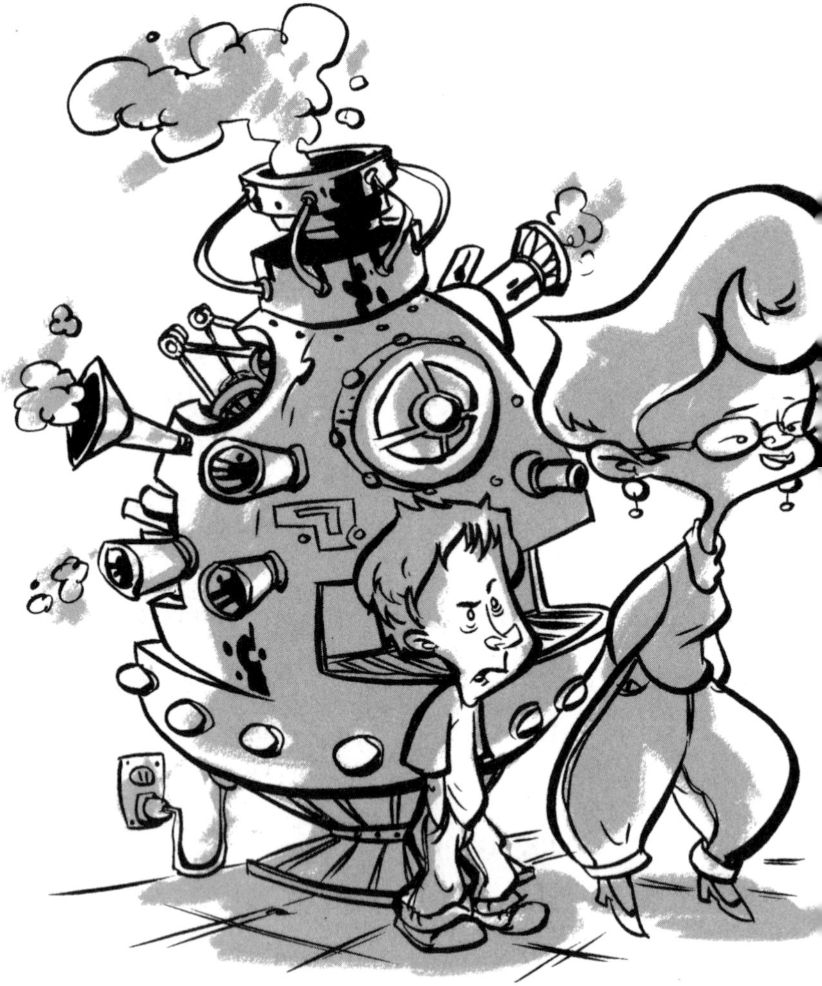

"**OOOOHHH!**" murmured the class.

"That is one weird-lookin' time machine," said Mikey.

"Look at those pipes and gears and switches and lightbulbs," said Jo Jo.

"Is that a coffeepot on top?" wondered Ellen. "And man, *it's huge!* I bet you could fit your *whole head* into one of those things!"

Next to the contraption sat a wagon filled with grapes. Ellen's eyes grew wide; she looked over to Jo Jo. Jo Jo recognized the grapes, too.

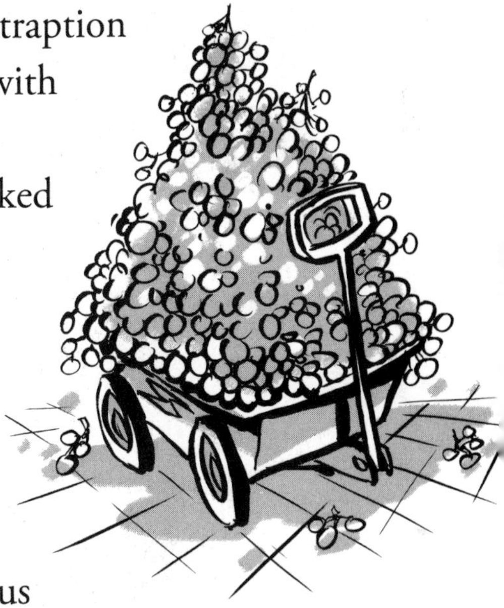

"My, my, Jarek, what an interesting invention! Can you tell us what it does?" asked Miss Emilyek.

Jarek knitted his brow and grinned a strange grin.

"He looks funny . . . like he did at the Farmers' Market," Jo Jo whispered to Ellen.

"I hope he doesn't freak out again."

"You've of course all heard of transmetrobolic hydrofusion?" Jarek asked the class. Jo Jo listened closely; most of the other kids looked confused. "My invention will replicate the diametric pentrosilius combustion present in all forms of transmutation, specifically during the transferal of solid materials into a state of liquefaction!"

Mikey Spuchins raised his hand. Jarek shot an evil look in his direction.

"So, um . . . can it travel through *just* time, or time *and* space?" asked Mikey.

"IT MAKES GRAPE JUICE!" Jarek shouted. He looked pretty impatient.

"Sourpuss," whispered Ellen.

Jo Jo looked worried.

"Ahem, all right, Jarek," said Miss Emilyek calmly. "Perhaps you'd like to give us a demonstration now?"

Jarek pushed a button on his invention.

Steam bellowed from the machine. Lights blinked and gears whirred. Jarek pulled out a screwdriver, made some adjustments to a knob, then turned a dial. His classmates watched eagerly, hypnotized by the machine.

Jarek carefully plucked a single grape from a bunch in the wagon next to the machine. He held it over the huge pipe on top of the machine. Mist formed.

"That gassy stuff on top looks like cotton candy at the state fair," said Ellen.

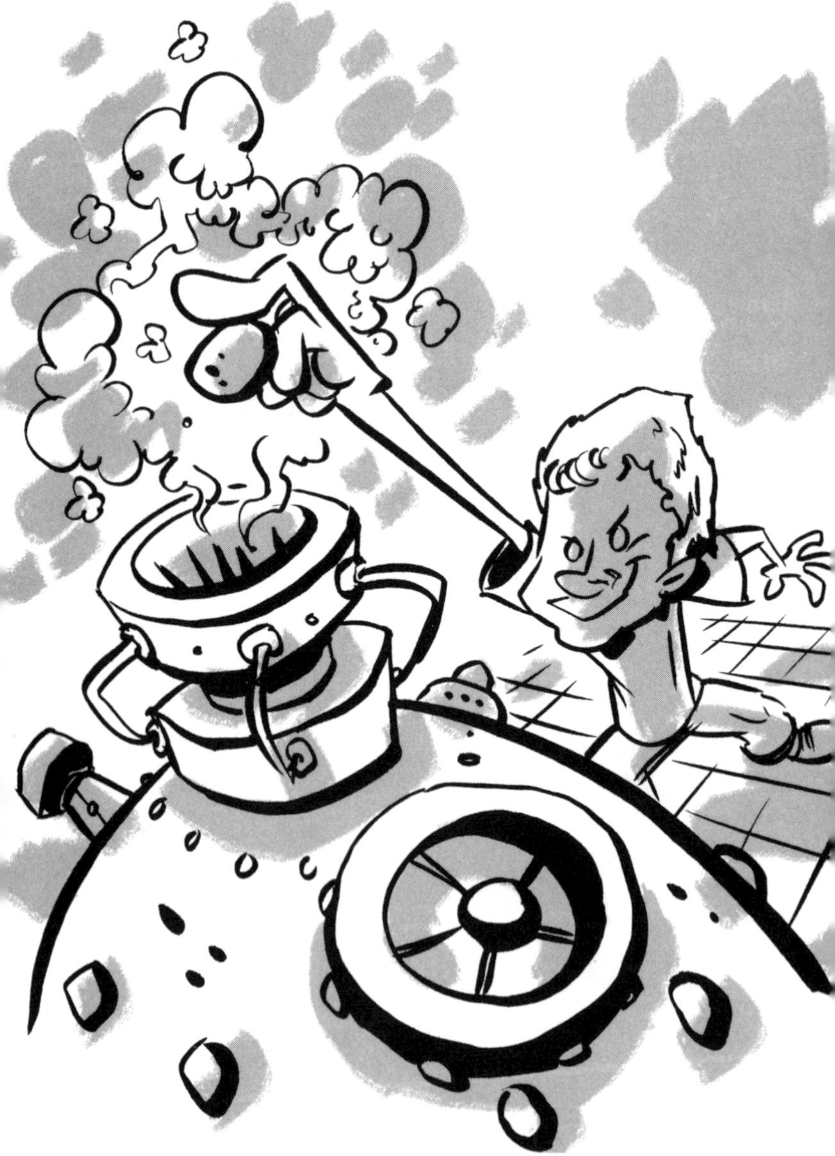

"I've got a bad feeling about this," muttered Jo Jo.

Jarek let go of the grape.

FWOOOOSH!

The grape disappeared into the swirling fog. The class leaned forward and stared. Jo Jo looked nervously at Ellen.

BBBBRRRIINNNNNGGGG!!!

The recess bell rang.

"He did it! He made time speed up!" shouted Mikey as he sprinted to the door. "Class flew by and recess is here!" The whole class headed for the door.

"Stop! How dare you evacuate the room during a show of my genius?!" Jarek cried. "You'll all beg for juice after recess! Mark my words!"

Chapter 7

DOOKLE DOOKLE DOOKLE!

The drinking fountain splurted water against Jo Jo's face.

"Ack!" she said and wiped her cheek with her sleeve.

"Here, let me show you how it's done," Ellen offered. She pushed past Jo Jo and gently twisted the knob. A slow stream of cool water trickled up; Ellen bent over and began to slurp.

FWOOOSHHHHHHHHHHHHHHH

A green streak flew past, flipping Ellen's hair over her head and right into the drinking fountain. Her hair got soaked.

"Awww, MAN!" cried Ellen. Stringy wet strands covered her face.

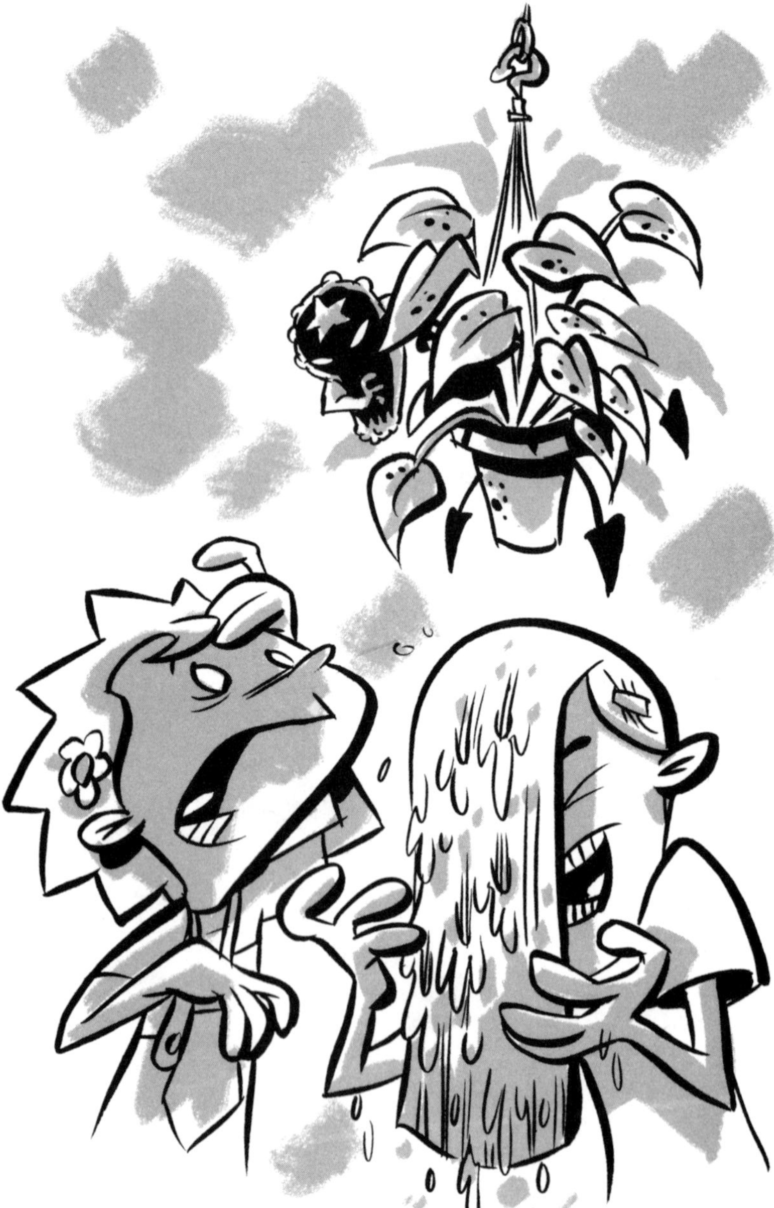

Jo Jo's eyes tracked the flash of green. It stopped and hovered near a hanging plant over Ellen's head.

The Magic Pickle blended in with the leaves almost perfectly.

"What are you DOING here?" Jo Jo blurted out.

"What's it look like?!" asked Ellen, tugging at the damp twisted strands covering her eyes. "I'm trying to SEE!"

Jo Jo looked around in a panic. Ellen couldn't see the Magic Pickle from underneath all her hair—he was doing a good job of staying hidden in the hanging plant—but someone might. One sharp look from some kid could blow the crime fighter's cover. The Magic Pickle kept silent, but Jo Jo could tell he wanted an update on Jarek.

"Someone might see you!" she whispered loudly.

"Well, I won't be able to see them!" Ellen

squealed. "It's all in my eyes! I probably look like I've got a mop on my head!"

The Magic Pickle's blue star glowed. It began to blink at Jo Jo: on, off, on, on, off, on, on, off.

"Oh, I get it!" Jo Jo whispered. "You're using some sort of code! Like Morse code or something!"

"Mop, mop, not *s'mores*!" Ellen said. "My hair probably looks like a *mop*!"

"Jarek built some kind of weird juice machine," Jo Jo whispered to the plant. "It's huge . . . big enough to make enough juice to flood the school, I bet."

The Magic Pickle's eyes widened. He was concerned.

"Who cares what Jarek built?!" cried Ellen. "What about my hair? It's never going to dry!"

Ellen finally brushed her tangled mess of hair away from her eyes.

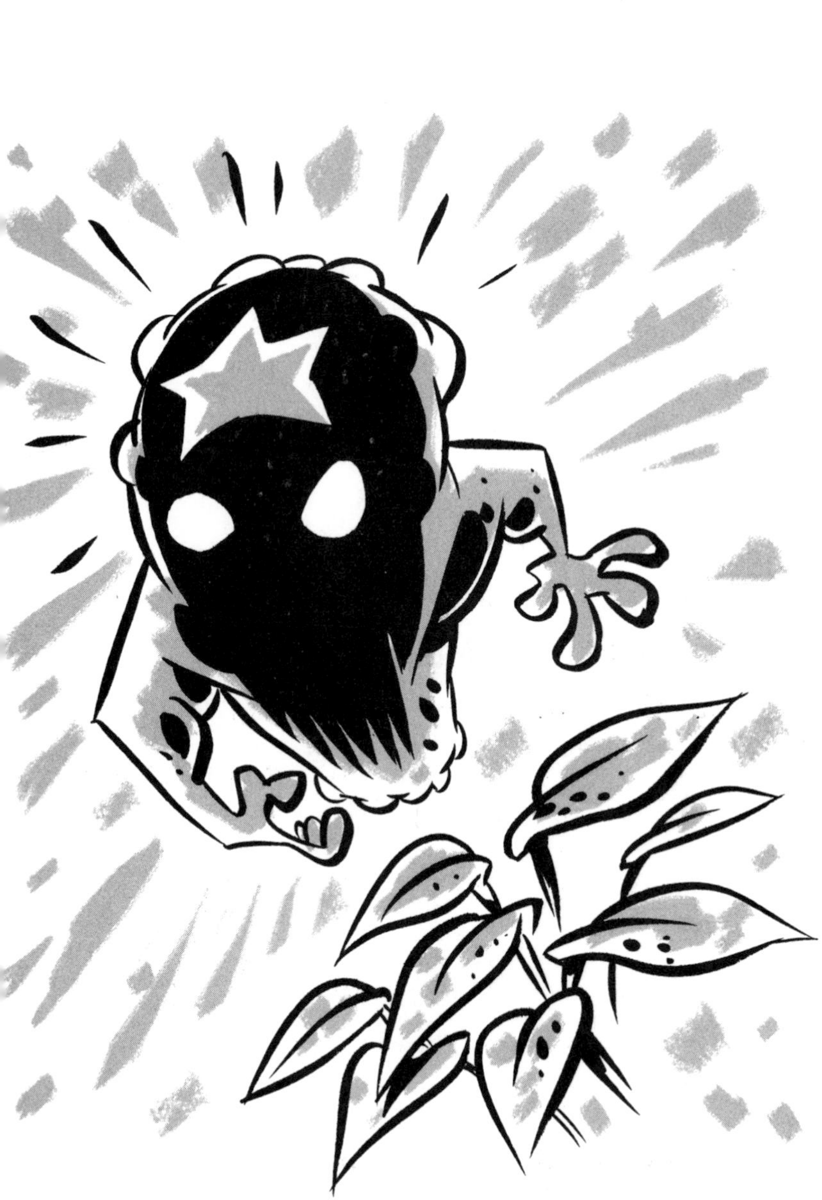

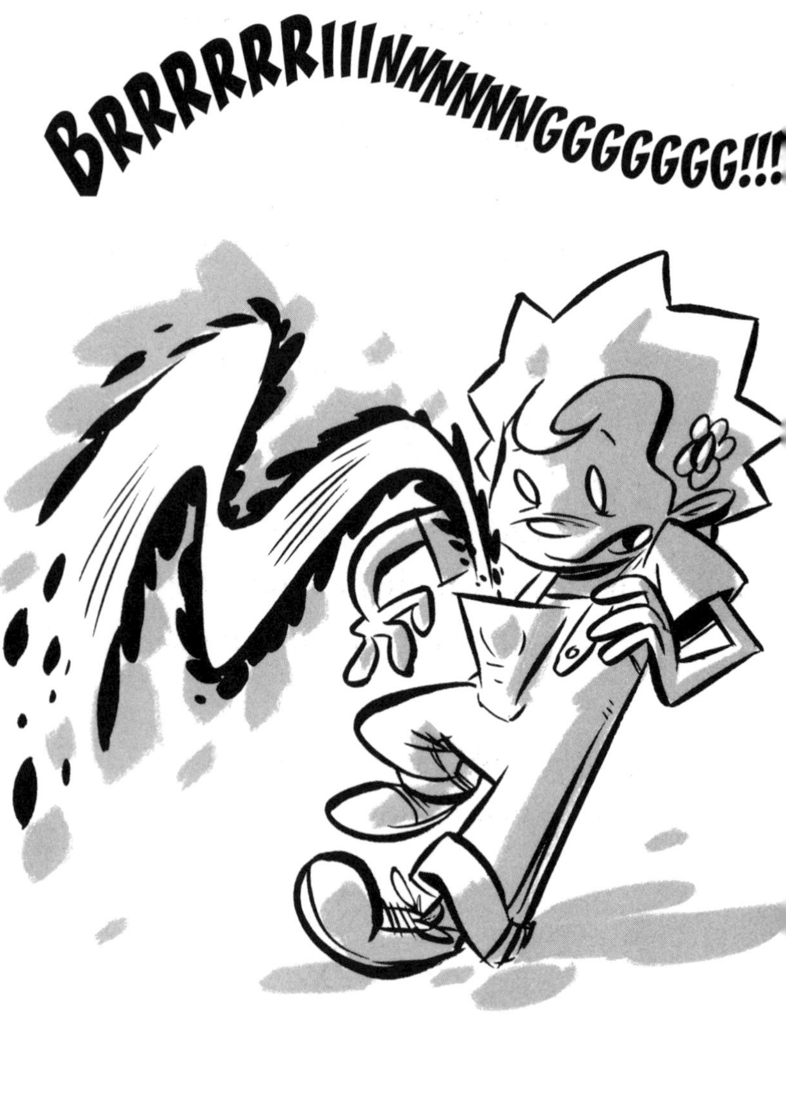
BRRRRRRRIIINNNNNNNGGGGGGG!!!

Jo Jo gasped. What if Ellen saw the Magic Pickle?

Just as Ellen turned, the Magic Pickle shot into the front pocket of Jo Jo's overalls.

"Don't forget me in here at laundry time," he said.

"Just my luck!" Ellen groaned. "I spend the whole recess just trying to get a drink and I'm still thirsty!"

"Well," said Jo Jo nervously, "maybe Jarek's machine will quench our thirst."

"Or at least blow-dry my hair," added Ellen.

The girls lined up with the rest of their class and headed inside.

Chapter 8

The class took their seats. Jarek walked around his machine. He checked dials and pressed buttons. He looked more sour than ever.

"You'll all be begging," Jarek muttered. "Just give me one more minute."

"He's still acting like a jerky know-it-all," Ellen whispered.

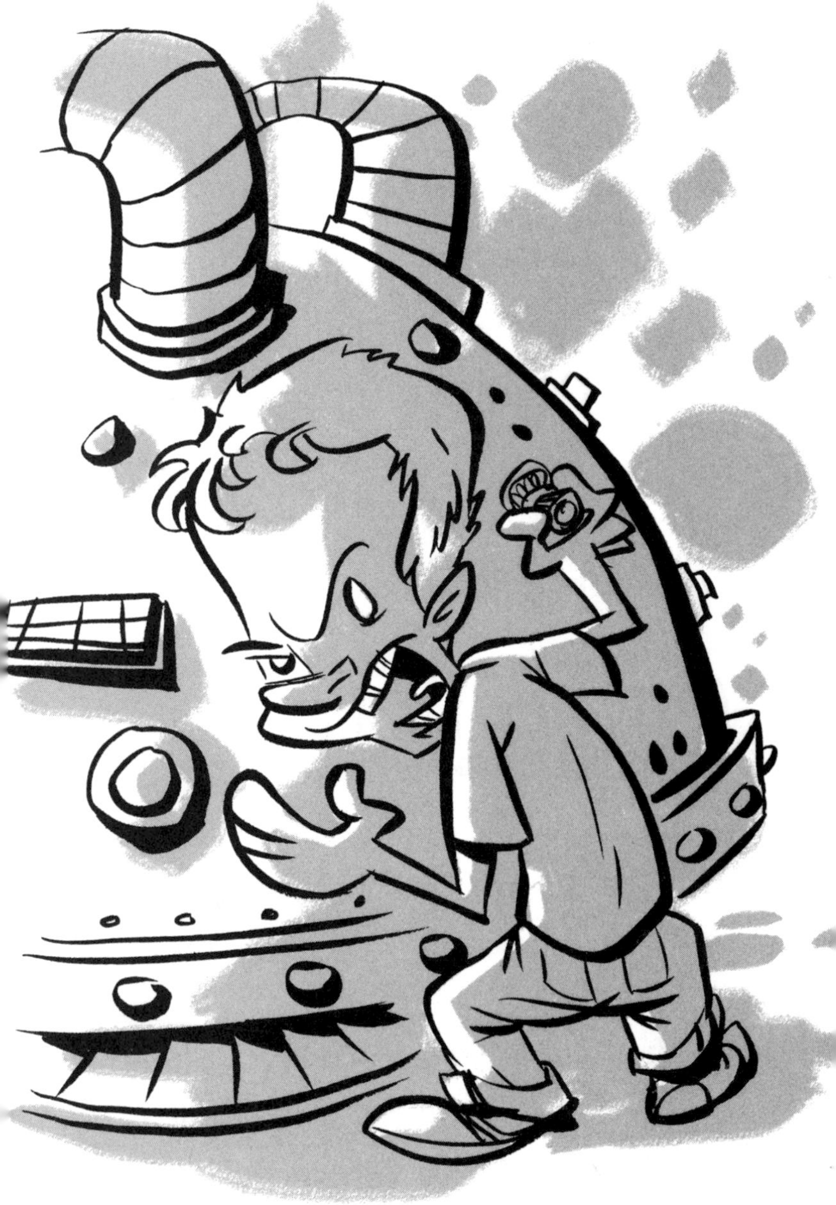

"He's getting on my nerves, that's for sure," Jo Jo agreed.

"Miss Emilyek?" called Lu Lu Deederly. She had her hand raised.

"Yes, Lu Lu?" Miss Emilyek asked.

"I just wanted to remind you that it's my turn to be the lunchroom helper," said Lu Lu.

"You're excused to go help Miss Vanderpants prepare the lunches," Miss Emilyek said.

Lu Lu swaggered toward the door. When she got near Jo Jo and Ellen's desks, she stopped.

"Oh, I almost forgot my strawberries," Lu Lu said with a grin. She grabbed them from out of her desk. "They'll go great with my lunch."

"She's getting on my nerves almost as much as Jarek," Jo Jo said as Lu Lu left.

The Magic Pickle peeked out of Jo Jo's

pocket and glanced at Jarek's machine. He squinted at the grape that floated above the big pipe on top of the machine. It bobbed and wavered in the swirling fog.

"We're close now," Jarek assured the class. He reached into his pocket, pulled out a piece of gum, unwrapped it and popped it in his mouth.

"Hey!" Ellen cried. "We're not allowed to chew gum in class!"

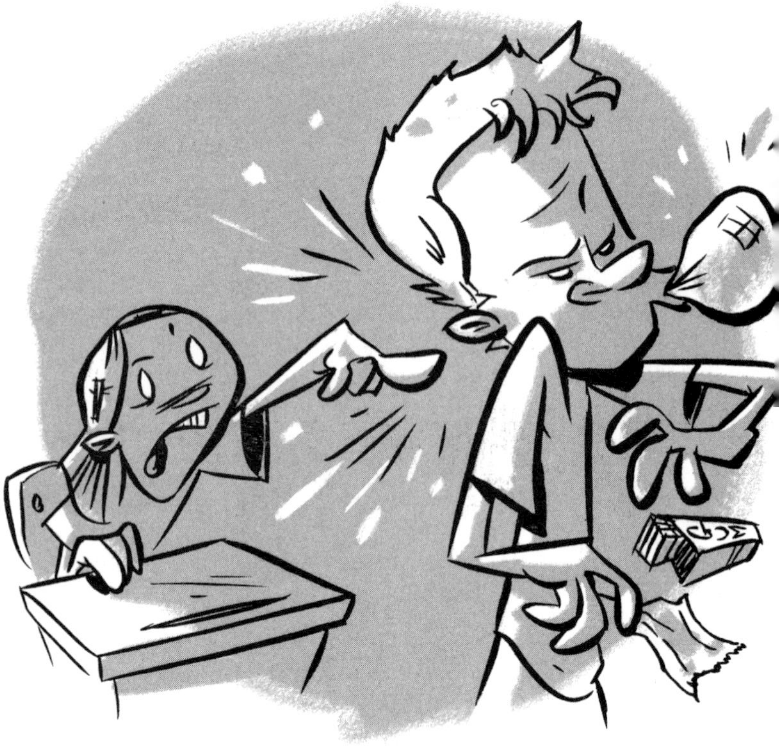

"Jarek! Spit out that gum this instant!" Miss Emilyek demanded. "You don't get special treatment just because you're up front today!"

Jarek's mouth fell open. The gum pack fell to the floor.

He looked worried. His attitude had completely changed.

"Oh man, what did I get myself into?" Jarek asked. He looked like he might start crying. "How did I build this thing? I don't remember anything since Sunday morning at the Farmers' Market!"

"Is he gonna squirt tears?" Mikey asked.

"Wow, he went from sour to softy in like three seconds flat," said Ellen.

Jo Jo looked down at the gum pack Jarek had dropped. It was Juicy Strawberry flavor.

"I think the sweet gum counteracted his sour puss!" Jo Jo said.

"Interesting," whispered the Magic Pickle. "It appears that sugar soothes the savage sour."

Just then, a whistle on top of the contraption began to blow.

"What's . . . what's going on?!" Jarek yelped.

Smoke shot out of the big pipe.

"That thing's like a furnace!" Mikey winced. "It's getting hot in here!"

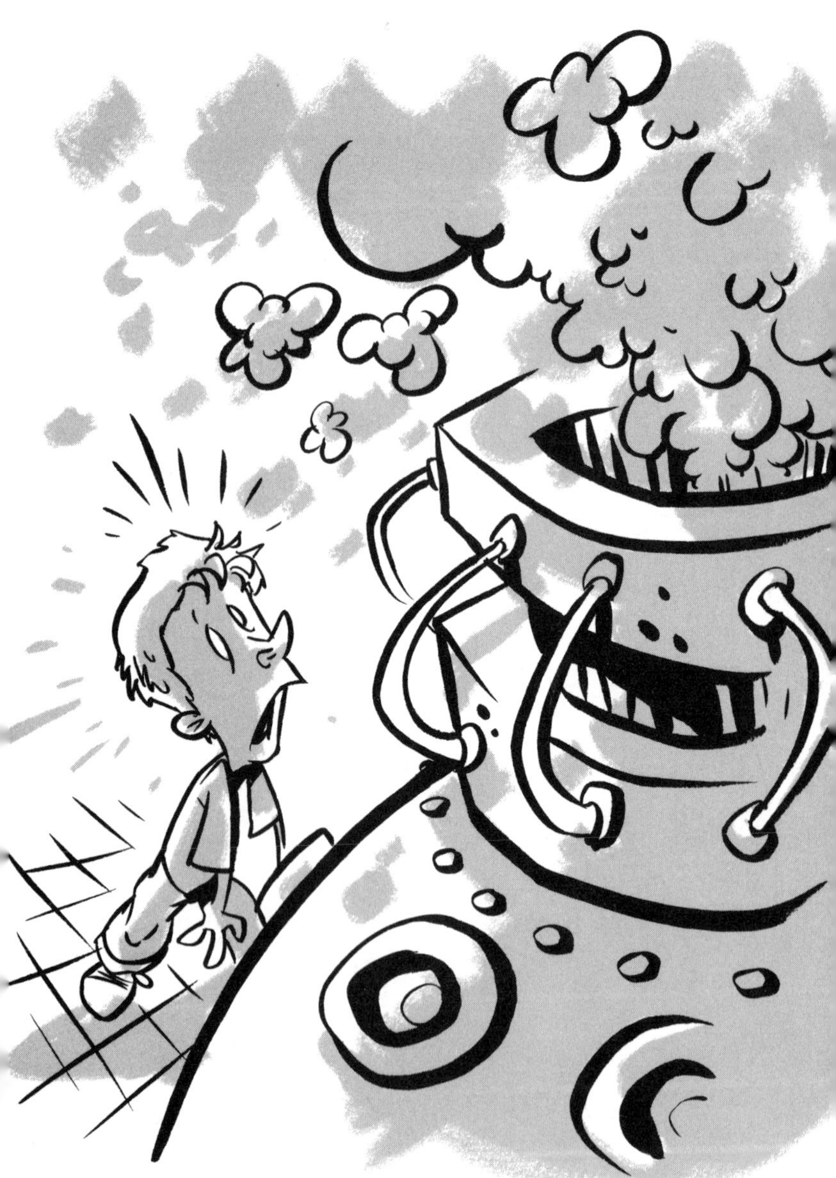

SSSPPPOOOONNNKKK!

The grape floating above the big pipe began to shrivel up.

"I thought we were gonna get juice!" a girl called from the back of the class.

"Looks like he's just making a big ol' raisin!" a boy complained.

"**AAAAAIIIIGGGHHHH!!!**" screamed the class. Miss Emilyek stood aghast.

A pulsing, wrinkly, purple grape with two strong-looking arms floated out of the steamy fog. Its eyes glowed. The shriveled grape grabbed Jarek by the wrist.

Jarek screamed.

The dried-up grape began to glow purple.

And laughed a crazy laugh.

"What's it going to do to Jarek?" asked Jo Jo.

"Hello, Jarek!" the raisin cackled. "You've done your job perfectly! My powers have

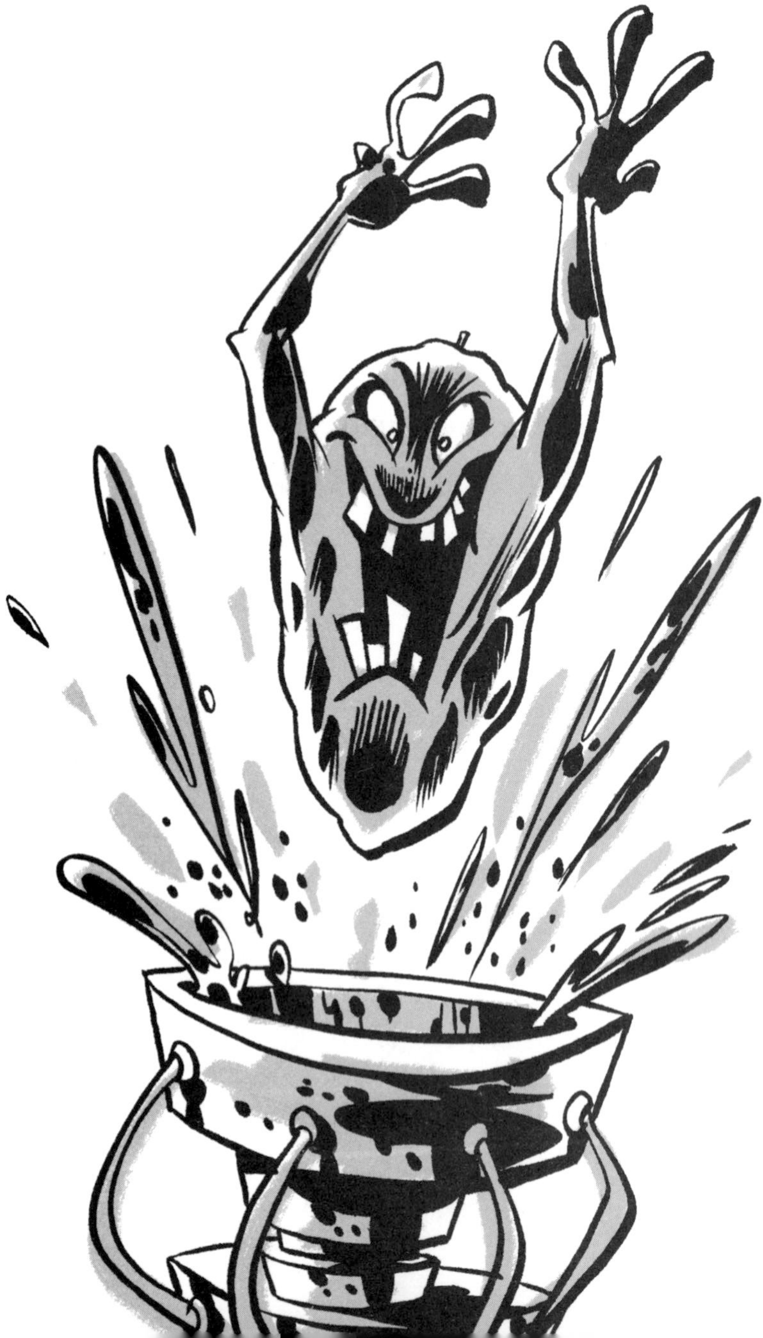

grown strong, my sun-dried, sour powers. Now the world will know the fury of The Razin'!"

Jarek shook from pure terror.

"What . . . what do you want from me . . . ?" he cried.

"Want? *I already got it*, Jarek!" answered The Razin'. "All I needed was your machine to switch on and bring me to power! I'm the newest food fighter of the Brotherhood of Evil Produce, and I'm going to turn every human being in your class . . . every human being in the WORLD . . . into *grapes*! A *Planet* of the Grapes!!! BWAHAHA!"

The Razin' grabbed grapes from beside Jarek's invention and flung them into the contraption. The grapes floated and glowed in a sticky ooze.

The Razin' pressed a button.

Grapes shot out of the machine and zipped through the air with perfect aim . . .

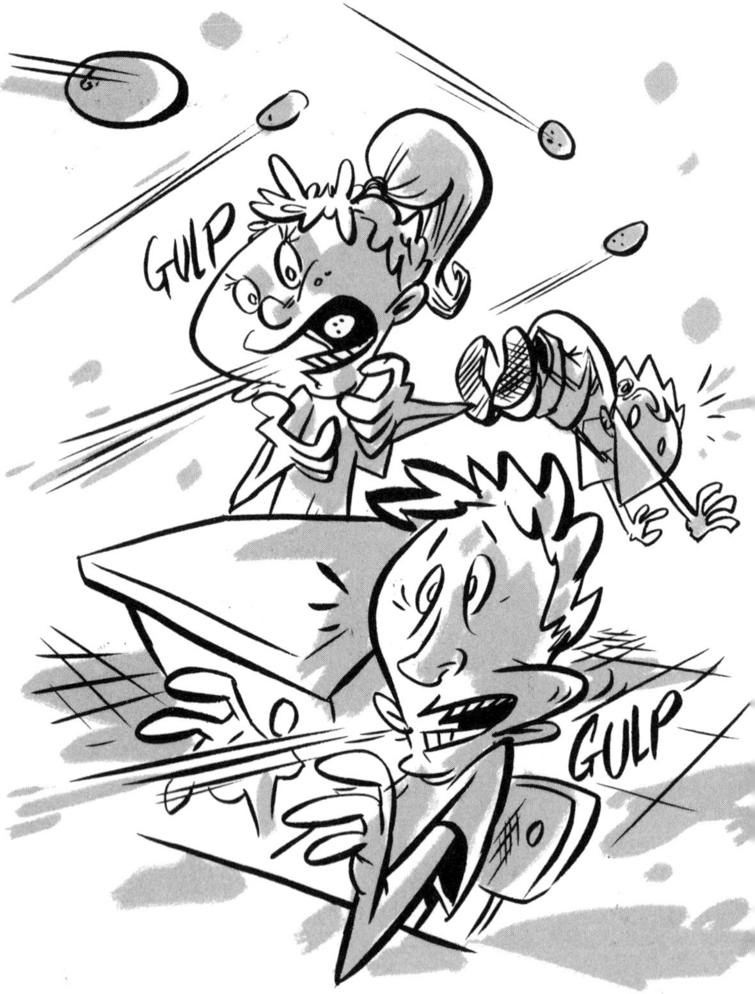
GULP
GULP

. . . right into the mouths of almost everyone in the class. Jo Jo jumped out of her chair and ducked just in time.

"Oof!" cried Jo Jo. She slammed into Jarek and they tumbled out of the way as grapes smashed against the chalkboard. The Magic Pickle shot out of Jo Jo's bib pocket like a rocket. He hid under a desk for cover.

"And now it's time to get *round*, people!" giggled The Razin'.

Kids began to swell up and roll out of their

BOIMP!

BOIMP!

BOIMP!

desk chairs. Miss Emilyek ran for the phone. By the time she reached it, she couldn't pick it up.

Jo Jo and Jarek huddled under two desks. They watched the whole class turn into big, round, purple, shiny grapes.

Ellen tried to hide in the coat closet.

"Oh, no!" cried Jo Jo—then quickly clamped her hand over her mouth.

FOOMP!

A grape shot out of the machine. It

bounced off the ceiling and then ricocheted off the classroom globe.

GLOOMP!

Before Ellen could close the coat closet door, she'd swallowed the grape.

BOIMP!

Ellen floated out of the open classroom door and down the hall. She was headed back toward the playground.

"**HEEE HHEE HE HEEEEE HHHAWWW!**" chortled The Razin'. "Most students want good grades, but today, all they're getting is good *grapes!*"

The Razin' scooped more drippy grapes out of the machine's gooey glass bowl. Jo Jo and Jarek huddled even tighter under the desk.

"Wouldn't it be grape if the whole school had a special treat with lunch?" The Razin' chuckled. He turned to leave.

SMACK!

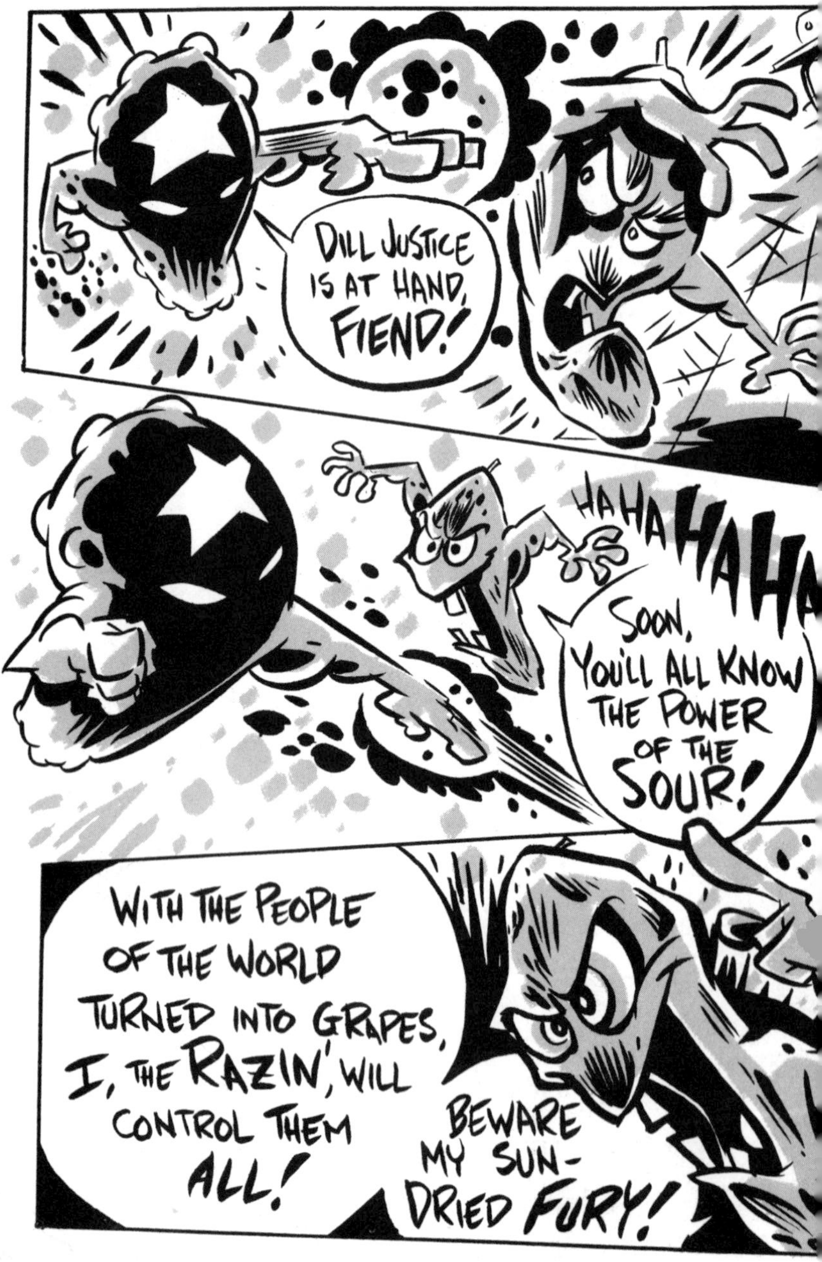
DILL JUSTICE IS AT HAND, FIEND!
HAHAHAHAHA
SOON, YOU'LL ALL KNOW THE POWER OF THE SOUR!
WITH THE PEOPLE OF THE WORLD TURNED INTO GRAPES, I, THE RAZIN', WILL CONTROL THEM ALL!
BEWARE MY SUN-DRIED FURY!

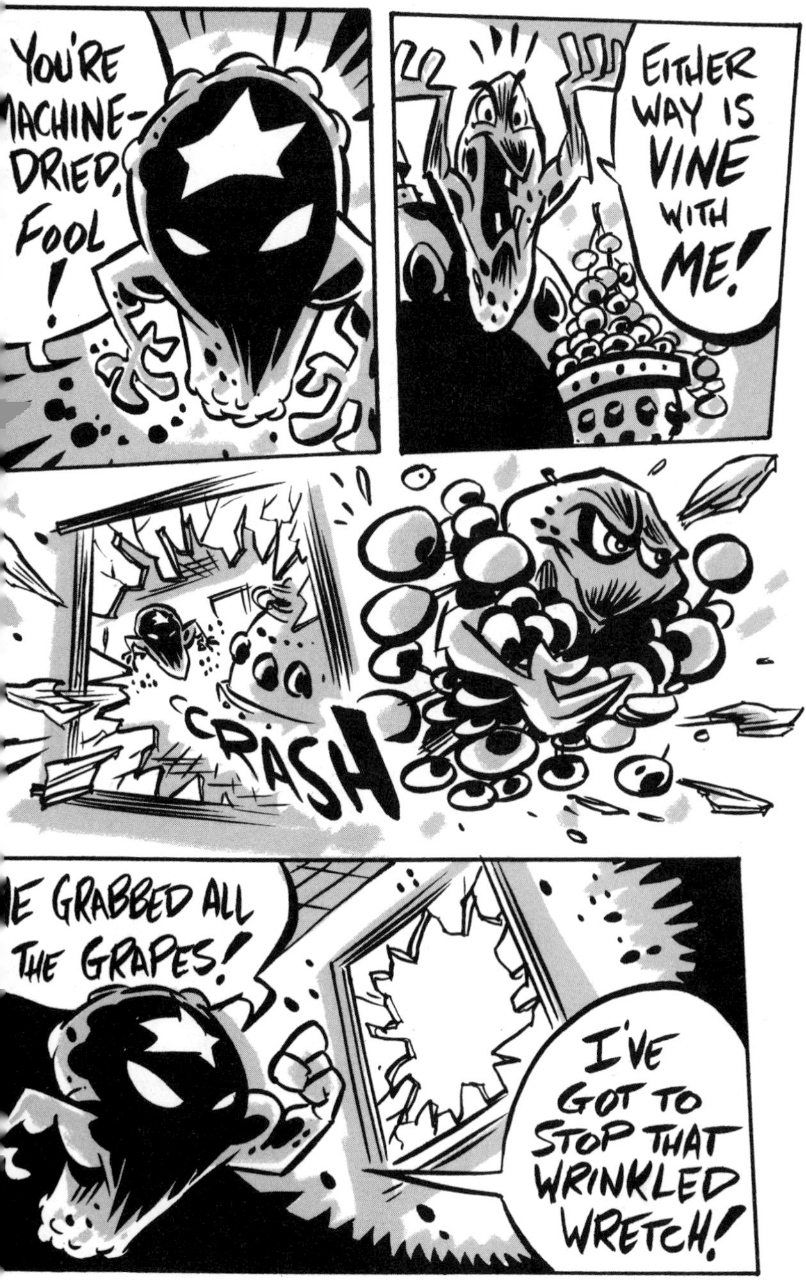
YOU'RE MACHINE-DRIED, FOOL!
EITHER WAY IS VINE WITH ME!
CRASH
E GRABBED ALL THE GRAPES!
I'VE GOT TO STOP THAT WRINKLED WRETCH!

Chapter 9

The classroom was a mess. Desks were overturned. Books were ripped apart. Giant grapes floated and bumped into each other. Even the classroom's pet hamster, Binky Alawicious, was loose. His cage was a twisted wreck.

"Punching purple . . . flying green . . ." Jarek was babbling.

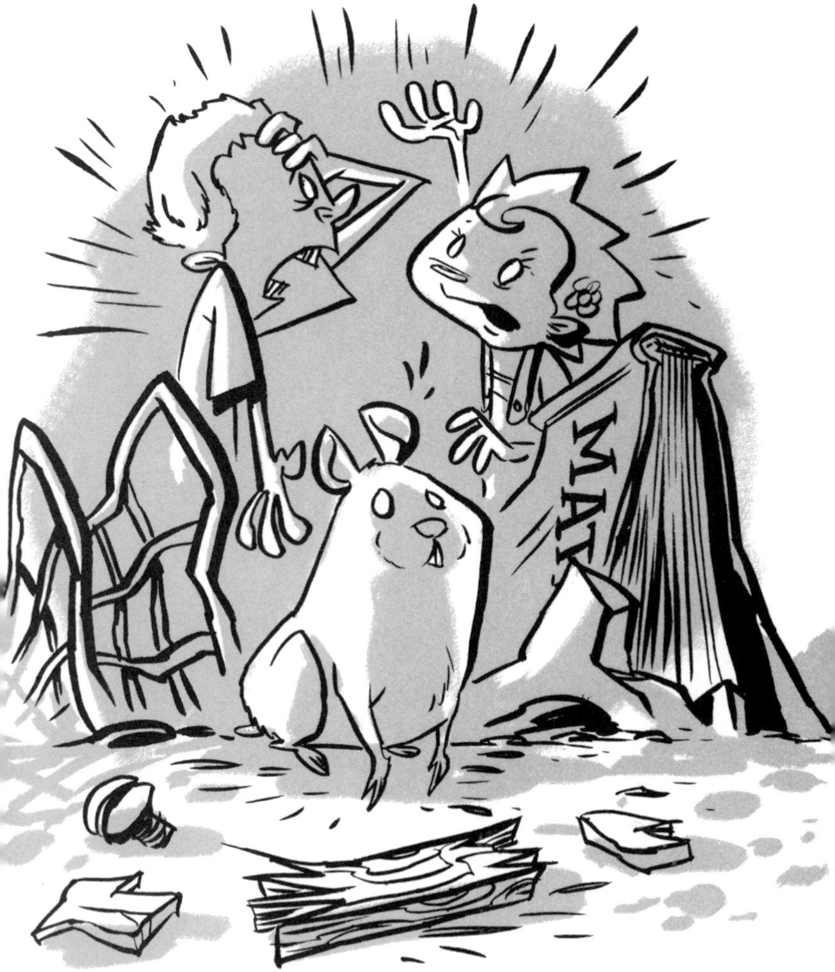
MAT

"Uh . . . quick! Better catch Binky," said Jo Jo to distract him.

"This is all my fault!" cried Jarek. "And I don't even remember how I did it or why! I tried to make a grape juice machine . . . but now that I think of it, something in my head told me to make it extra sour."

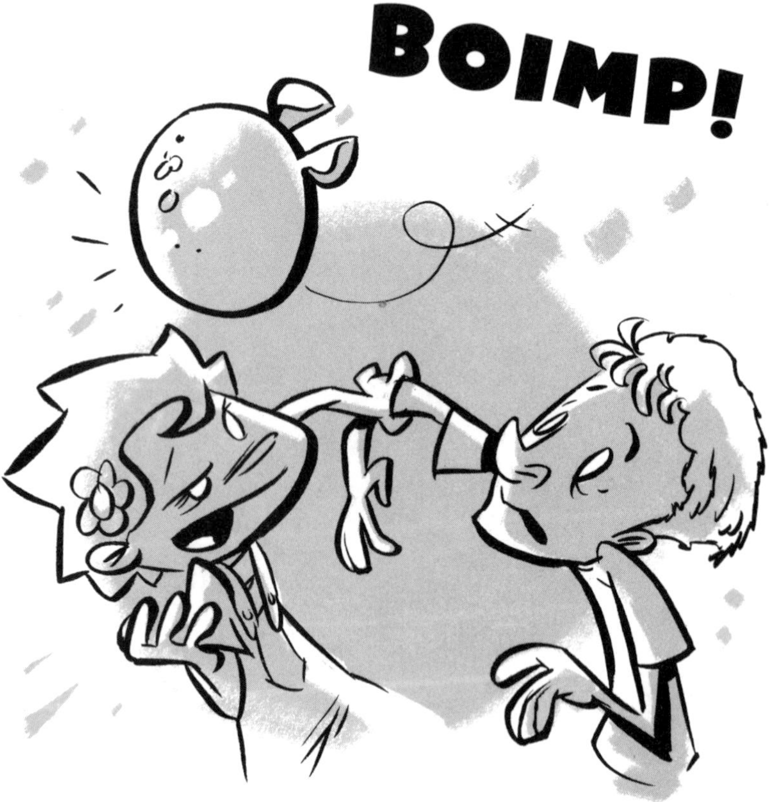
BOIMP!

"That was the bad lemonade you drank at the Farmers' Market," explained Jo Jo. "It wasn't your fault. The Brotherhood of Evil Produce must have left it as a trap, to turn people into sourpusses."

"The Brotherhood of *what?*" asked Jarek.

"Watch out!" cried Jo Jo. A gooey grape rolled out of the tube on the machine. Binky Alawicious grabbed it and nibbled.

Binky floated past the two kids. He had turned into a grape the size of a football. "Yikes!" gasped Jarek.

"You know it's time to go when you've seen a fruit-flavored hamster," Jo Jo said. She grabbed Jarek by the arm. Together, they stumbled past their big, round, purple classmates and out the classroom door.

"Where are we going?" asked Jarek.

"We've gotta jam," said Jo Jo.

Chapter 10

Lu Lu Deederly stacked cartons of milk onto lunchroom trays. This was part of her job as a lunchroom helper. She also got to eat her lunch early.

"Well, I still think people would like a choice between milk or juice," Lu Lu said with a sneer.

Miss Vanderpants, the lunchroom supervisor, turned toward Lu Lu and sighed.

"Just put the milk cartons on the trays next to the grapes, Lu Lu," she suggested. "Milk's a healthier choice."

"Oh, I'm very health conscious," Lu Lu assured her. "I even brought my own fruit today, organic strawberries from the Farmers' Market."

Miss Vanderpants tried to ignore Lu Lu as they prepared trays and ate their lunches.

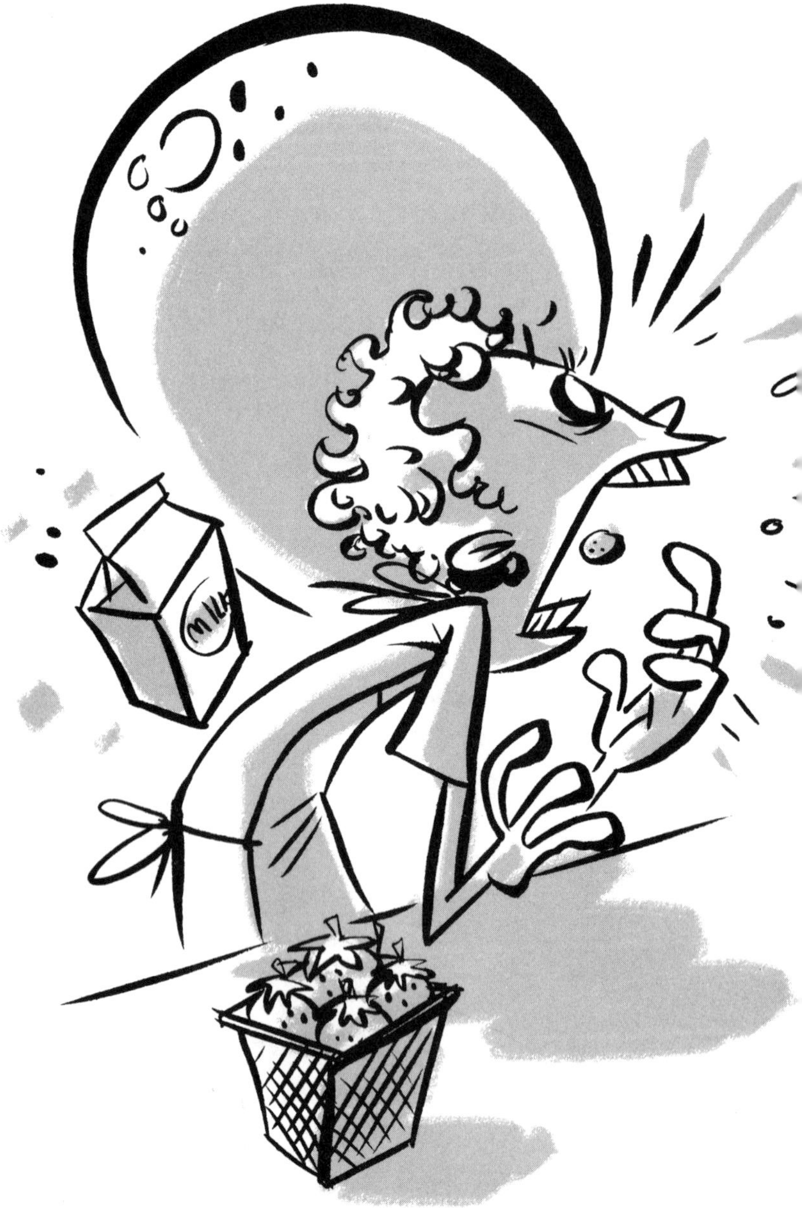
MILK

Lu Lu sucked strawberry after strawberry into her mouth, the juice spilling down her chin. Miss Vanderpants continued to pull bunches of grapes out of a nearby bowl and put them on the lunch trays.

"Strawberries make you sweeter," explained Lu Lu to Miss Vanderpants. "You know, sweeter like me. You should try one." Miss Vanderpants raised an eyebrow. She tossed a grape into her mouth. As she bit into her grape, she started to change. Her face grew plump. Her skin grew shiny.

In the blink of an eye, Miss Vanderpants turned into a giant grape.

Lu Lu hadn't noticed, though. She was too busy popping strawberries in her mouth. Her eyes were closed as she enjoyed the juicy berries.

"**AAAIIIGGGGHHHH!**" screamed Lu Lu. Her eyes flew open as she bit down on a grape.

"GROSS! I did NOT pay for that with my strawberries!" she said.

"Consider it a free sample," said a raspy voice.

Lu Lu looked up; The Razin' floated in front of her face, holding a strawberry. He'd snatched it out of her basket and switched it for one of his gooey grapes.

BOIMP!

Lu Lu, now a big ol' grape, rolled out the cafeteria door after Miss Vanderpants.

BRRRRIIINNNNGGG!

The lunch bell rang. Soon, kids from all over the school would fill the cafeteria. The Razin' smiled as he prepared the lunch trays. Each tray had a very special fruit cup on it— a fruit cup filled with gooey grapes!

"**BWAHAHAHAHAHAHA!**" chuckled The Razin'. "Every kid in school will be like a piece of fruit plucked from my vine of evil! What a vine, vine plan! I will vinely rule this planet of the grapes."

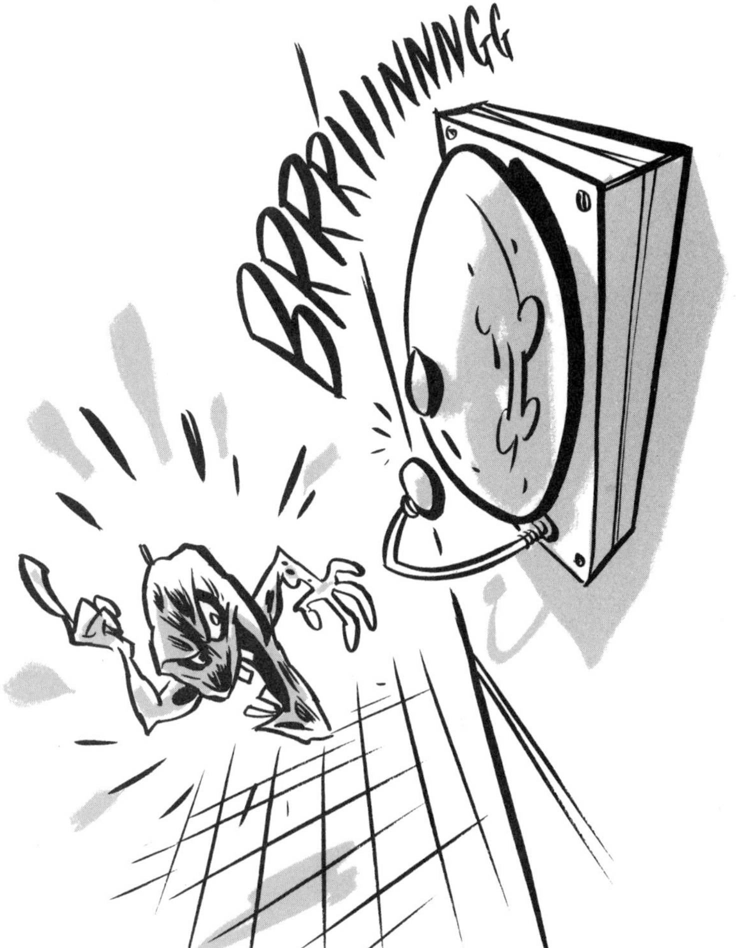
BRRRIIIINNNGG

Chapter 11

Jo Jo and Jarek ran across the playground. Three big grapes rolled by but no one else seemed to be around.

"Where is everyone? It's like a ghost town!" said Jarek.

"Except for those three big ol' grapes. One of them's Ellen, I think, but I don't know about the other two. Razin's struck again!"

Jo Jo groaned. "Everyone else is probably in the cafeteria. We've gotta warn them!"

Jo Jo and Jarek threw open the cafeteria doors.

The room was filled with grapes. ENORMOUS grapes.

"It's too late!" cried Jarek. "It's like a vineyard for giants in here!"

"It's never too late, Jarek!" tittered a voice from above. "Never too late to join my legion of juicy warriors! I call them the Grapes of Wrath!"

Jo Jo screamed, "How did you do this, you crazy raisin?!"

The Razin' sneered at her. "Why, I simply switched the grapes in the cafeteria with the juiced-up grapes from Jarek's machine! The whole school came in for lunch, and everyone who ate a grape is now under my control! I am the wisest grape, after all, aged to perfection, a natural-born leader! They'll follow my every wish!"

RUMBLE RUMBLE RUMBLE RUMBLE

Jarek and Jo Jo looked up to see The Razin', his eyes glowing purple, his twisted, crooked teeth dripping purple spit. He raised a crooked, purple finger at the grapes.

"ATTACK!" ordered The Razin'.

The humongous grapes began to shake and roll—right toward Jo Jo and Jarek!

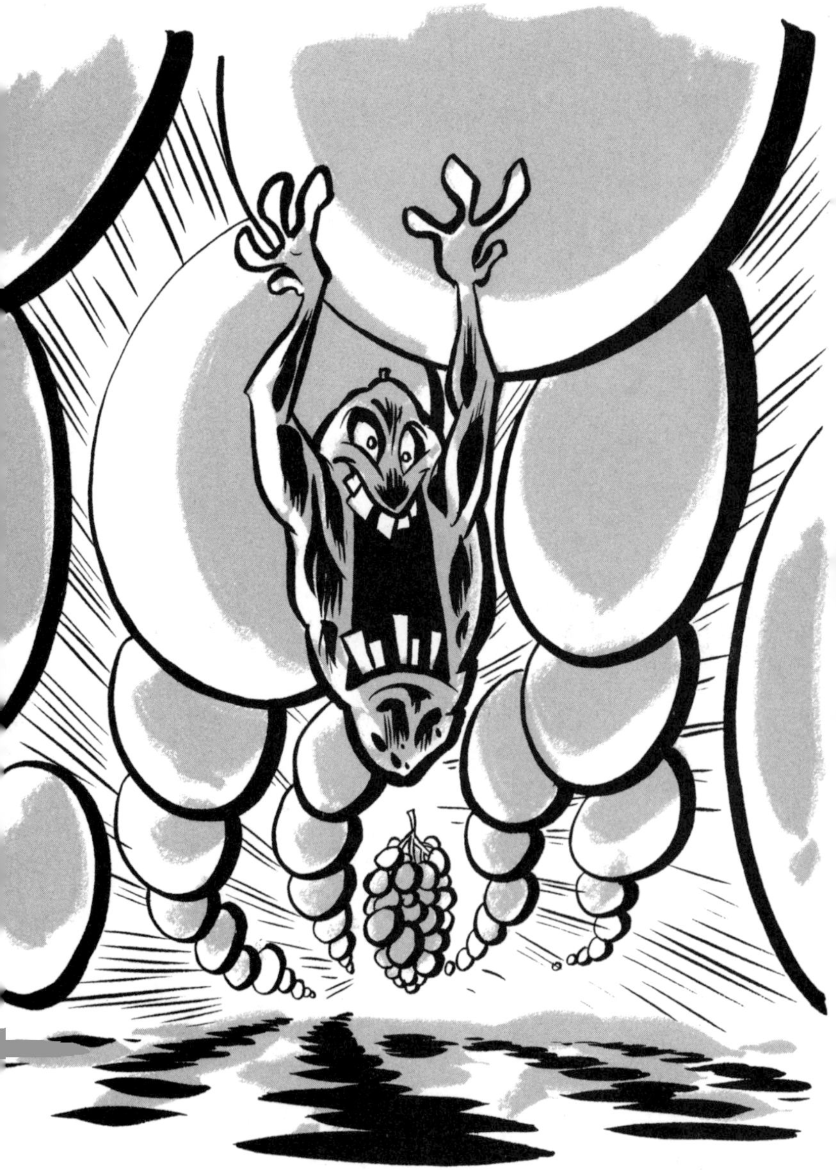

They ran through the cafeteria doors and out onto the playground. The army of grapes followed.

CCCRRRAAASSSHHH!!!

Some of the grapes were too big to fit through the doors. They burst through the cafeteria windows and dropped onto the playground.

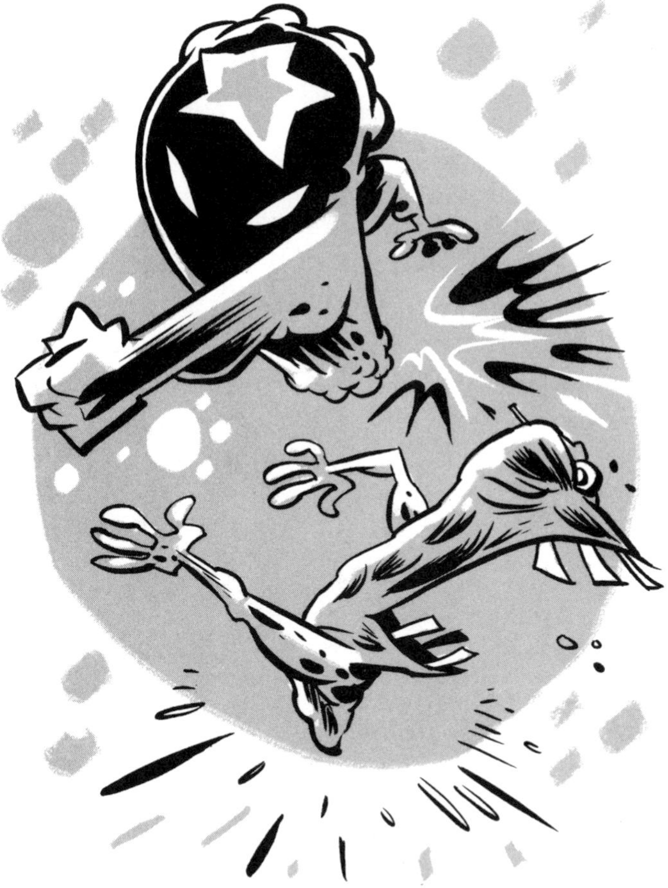

SQUELCH!

The Razin' hit the ground, floored by a vinegar-veined punch.

"Back off, Razin'," the Magic Pickle snarled, "or I'll whip you into a fruit smoothie!"

The Razin' shot into the air in a purple flash. He waved his hand through the air. The huge grapes formed a line and stood at attention, like a big purple army.

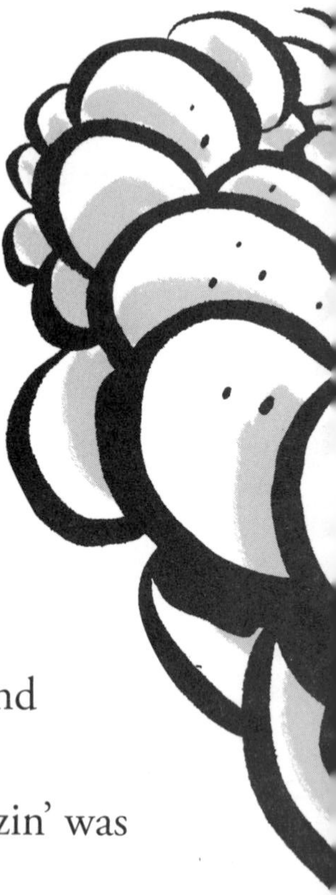

"Perhaps you've heard of the Great Wall of China?" The Razin' asked the Magic Pickle. "Well, meet the Grape Wall of The Razin'!"

"Let's go get the principal," said Jo Jo.

The Razin' waved his hand and the giant grapes rolled forward all at once. The Razin' was well protected.

"I'm afraid your wall has been condemned," said the Magic Pickle, "and I'm the wrecking ball!"

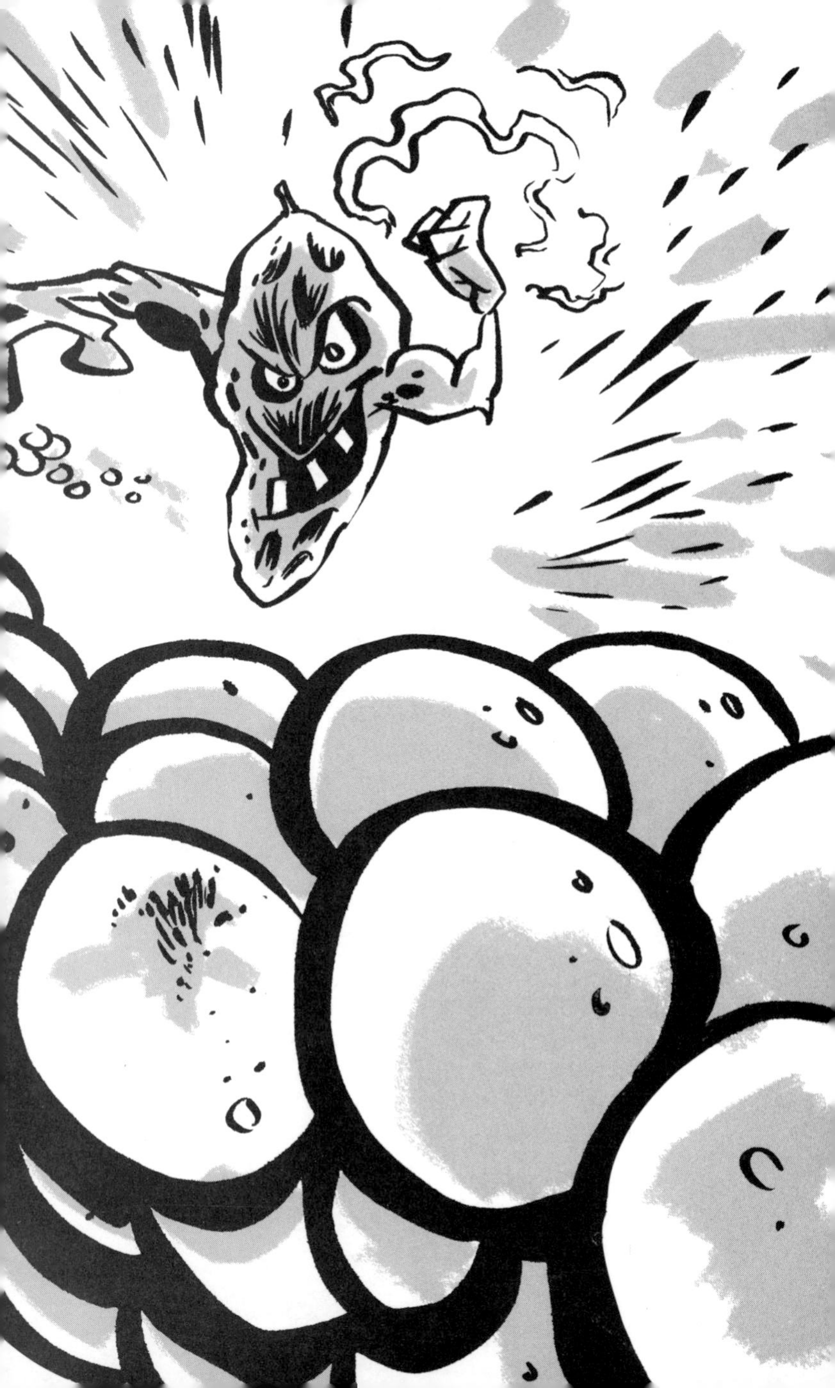

The Magic Pickle grunted and flew at the wall of grapes, his green fists held out like battering rams.

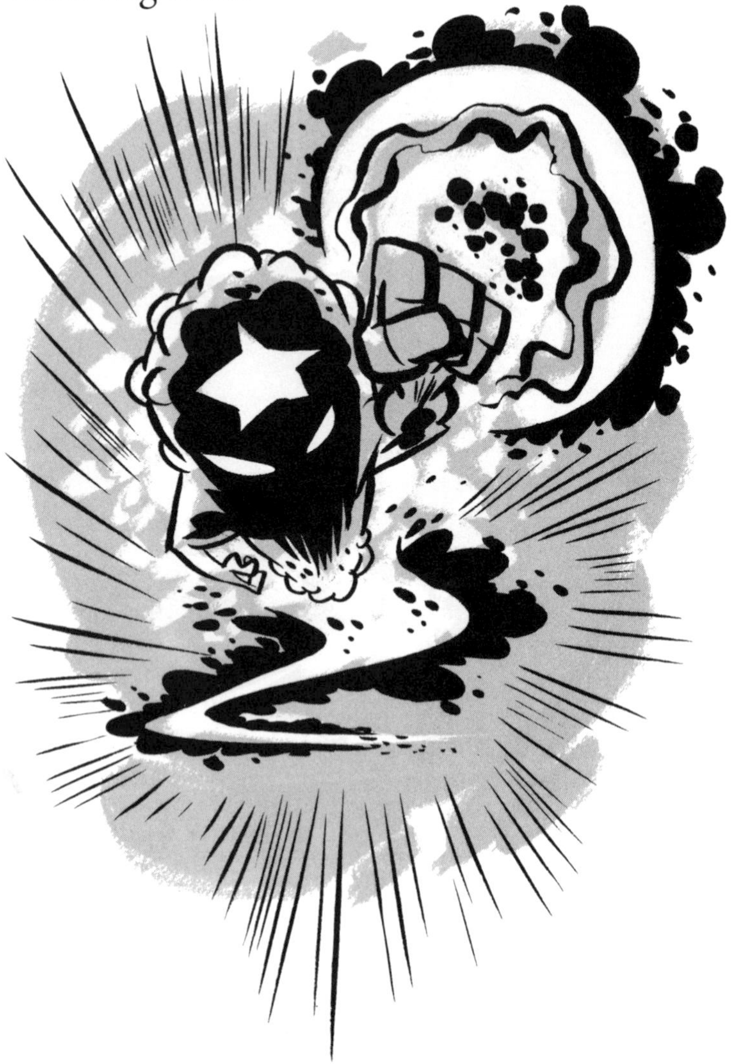

Chapter 12

"What the heck's going on?!" cried Jarek. "There's a flying pickle fighting a talking raisin! Am I going nuts?!"

BANG!

The principal's office door flew open. Out rolled more huge grapes.

"Principal Weatherall! The school secretary! Oh no!" cried Jarek.

The grapes rolled past Jo Jo and Jarek and joined the battle against the Magic Pickle.

"We've got to help the Magic Pickle stop that crazy raisin!" Jo Jo shouted.

"Wait, you *know* the pickle? This is getting weirder every minute!" said Jarek.

A bunch of grapes in the playground rolled right past Jo Jo and Jarek into the girls' *bathroom*.

WHOOSH!

All the toilets flushed at once. Jo Jo giggled.

"C'mon, let's get out of here!" said Jarek.

"Those are some real sour grapes!" she said. "If only we had something sweet, we might be able to balance out their sourness!"

Jo Jo looked down at her feet. She'd stepped in something squishy—a nice, plump, juicy strawberry.

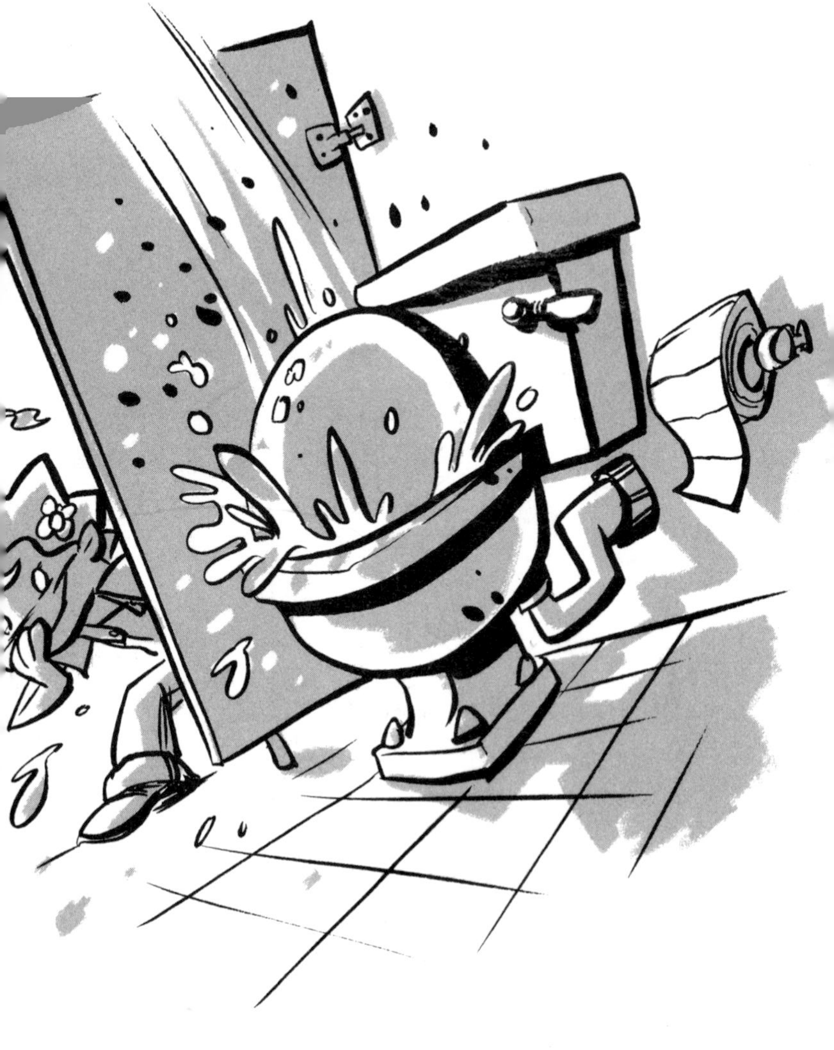

SQUORCH!

A *sweet* strawberry.

"Jarek, LOOK!" Jo Jo cried, picking up a strawberry. "These are Lu Lu's strawberries from the Farmers' Market!"

"Her basket must have overturned when

things went all fruity inside!" said Jarek. He picked a strawberry up and smelled it.

Just then, a huge grape rolled toward them.

"AAAHHHH!!!" screamed Jarek.

Thinking fast, Jo Jo threw a strawberry at the looming grape—it was all she had. Jarek ducked.

BOIMP!

BOIMP!

The juicy strawberry hit its grape target . . . and something magical happened.

The grape turned back into Mikey Spuchins!

"Oh, WOW!" Jo Jo exclaimed. She grinned and grabbed a handful of strawberries off the ground. She ran back toward their classroom.

"What are you doing?" screamed Jarek.

"Follow me!" shouted Jo Jo over her shoulder. "I've got a *berry* good feeling about this! It's gonna be SWEET!"

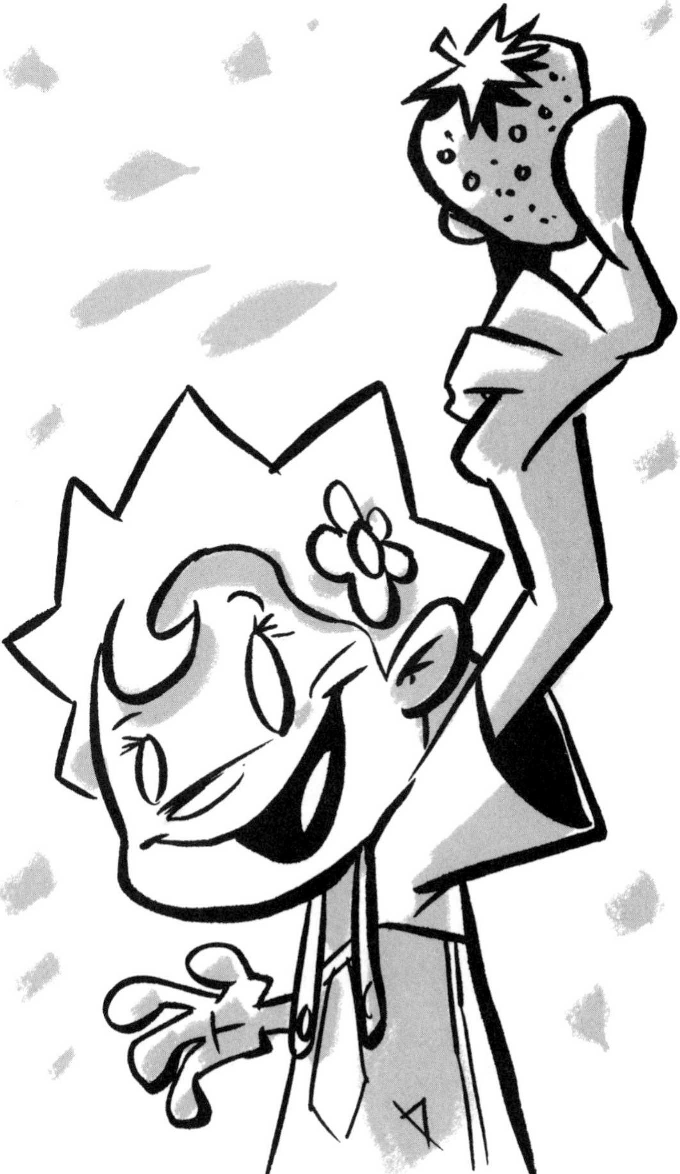

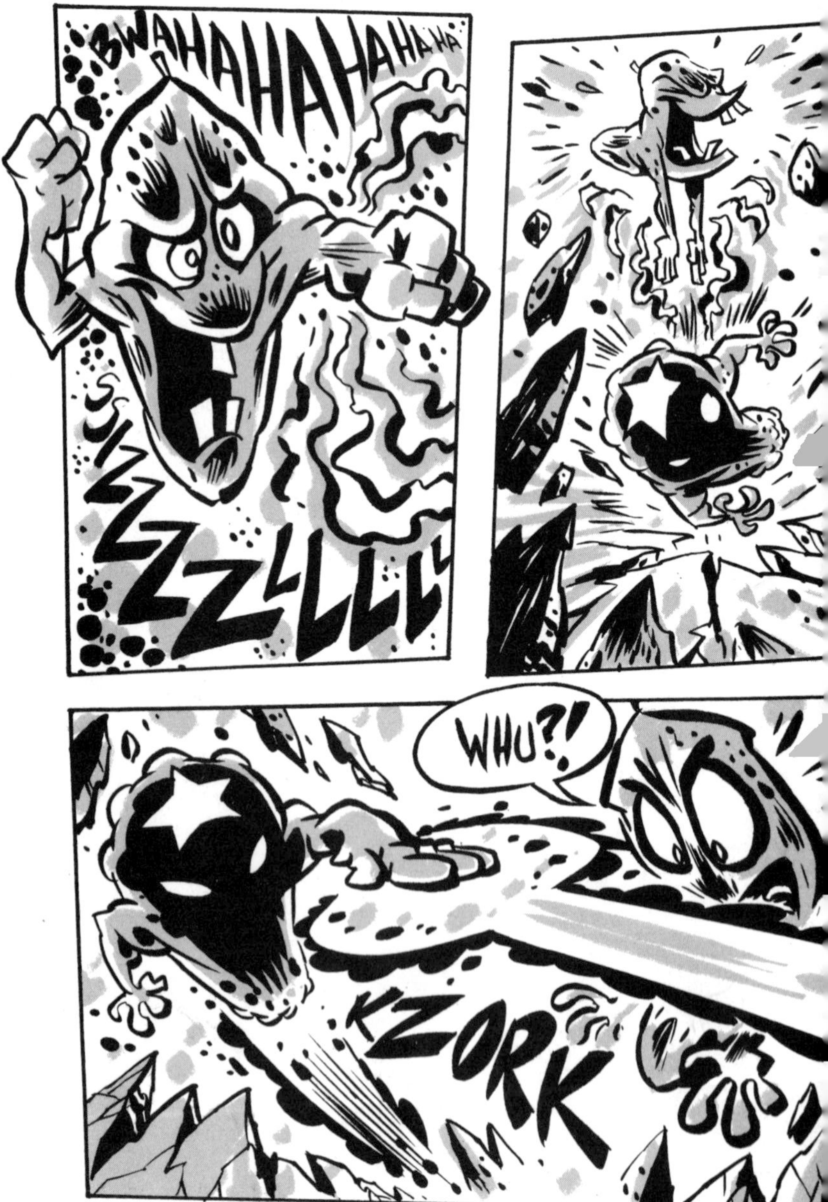
BWAHAHAHAHAHAHA
ZZZLLLLL
WHU?!
KZORK

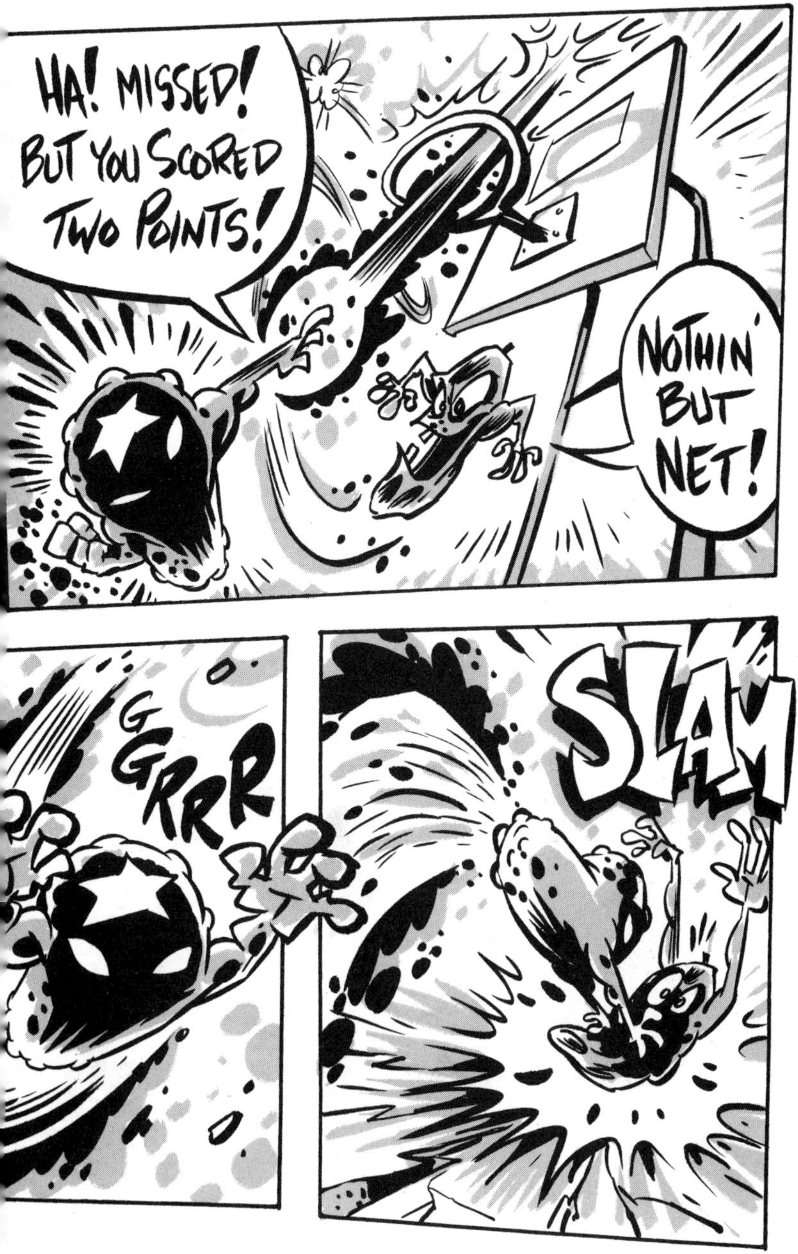
HA! MISSED! BUT YOU SCORED TWO POINTS!
NOTHIN' BUT NET!
GGRRR
SLAM

Chapter 13

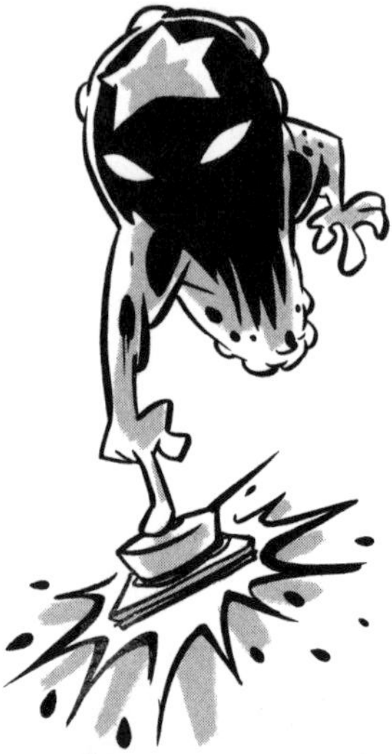

KERZERRRRKKK!!!

"WWWWAAAAAHHH!!!" shouted the Magic Pickle. The Razin' had zapped him good with a grapey energy bolt.

"HHHEEEEEEHEHEHEHEHEEEE!" giggled The Razin'. "No one can withstand the tart fury of my Grape Punch!"

The Magic Pickle rolled onto the ground, stunned.

He lifted himself on his elbows and looked up.

"The Age of Dehydration is near, Weapon Kosher." The Razin' chuckled. "When I'm done, you'll be drained of every ounce of vinegar that pulses through your bumpy green skin! You'll be a withered husk, like me! Maybe then you'll be able to relate to my wrinkled genius. . . . " .

The Razin' hovered above the Magic Pickle. Surges of purple energy crackled around The Razin's upraised arms.

"Your day in the sun has come to an end, you bumpy old gherkin. Now, it's time for Razin'!" The Razin' pointed at the Magic Pickle, ready to deliver a final burst of Grape Punches.

WWWHHHIIIIRRRRRRRRRR!!!...

Suddenly, a strange noise filled the playground. It was like a strong wind, only stranger. It sounded like a vacuum.

"You're overripe, you old prune!!" shouted Jo Jo.

The Razin' spun around, his grin turning to a look of dread.

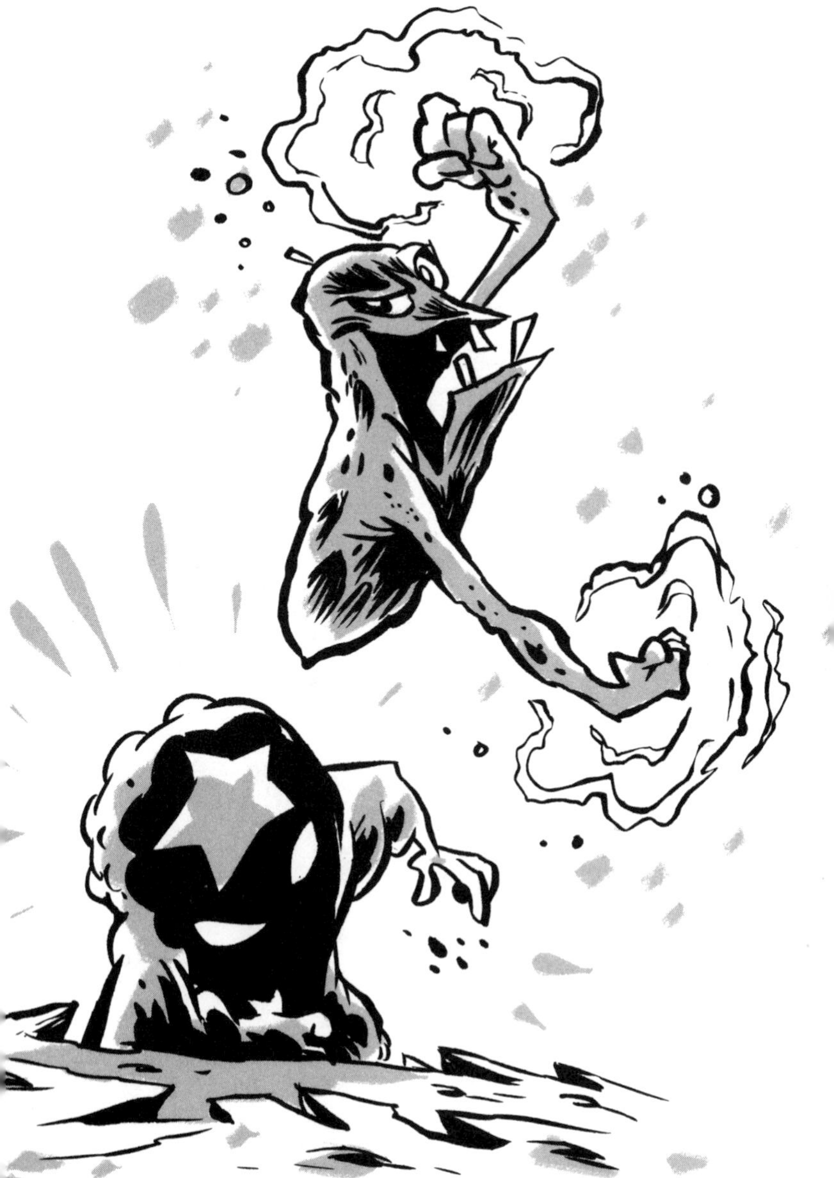

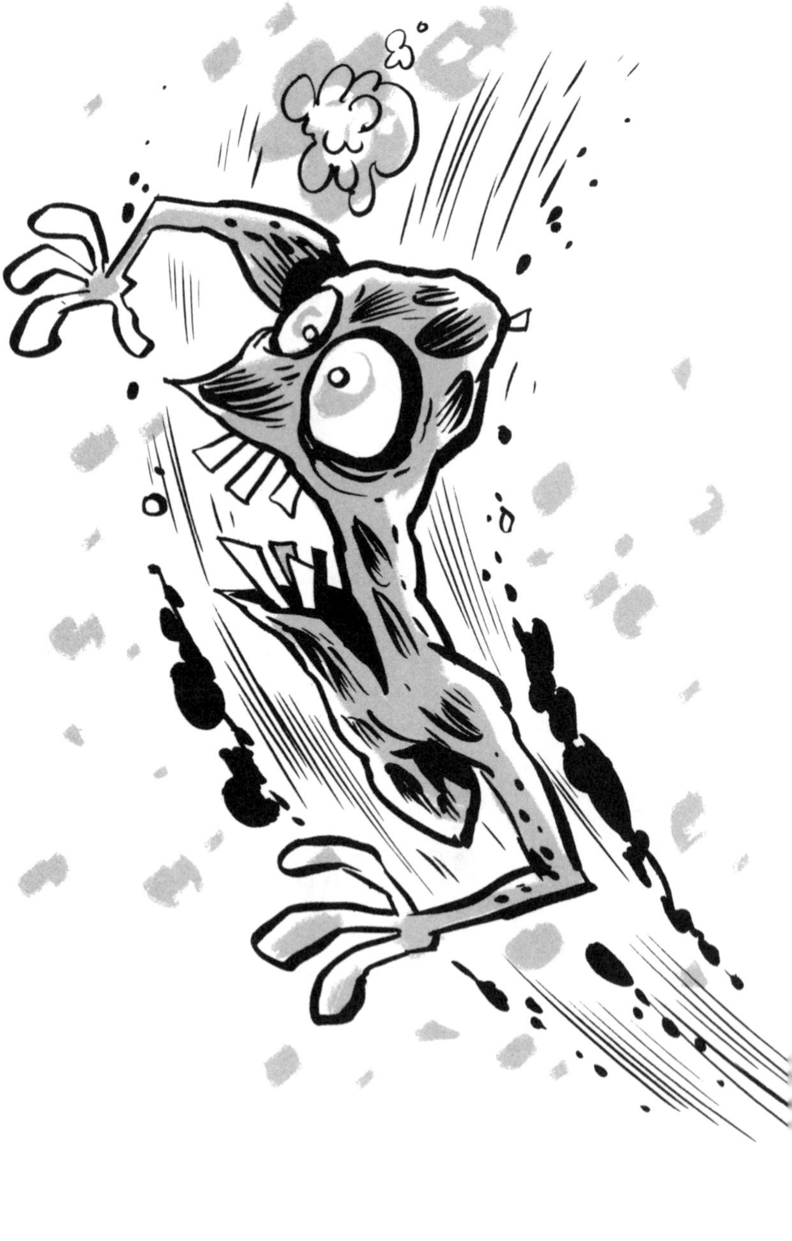

"It's time to make sure your fruity plans never come to fruition!" added Jarek.

Jo Jo and Jarek stood near Jarek's big machine.

"Interesting!" said the Magic Pickle when he saw the big pipe of churning pink smoke near the top of the machine. Pink juice squirted down tubes like sweet, sticky fuel.

CHUGGACHUGGACHUGGA FWWWOOOOOOMMMMM!!!

A huge vent sucked air into the machine.

"No . . . NOOO!!!" screamed The Razin'.

The vent pulled at the air harder and harder, sucking The Razin' closer and closer . . . until Jarek's invention, the same invention that made him . . . swallowed him whole!

The Razin' disappeared into the machine.

A big puff of purple smoke bellowed out, then a small grape rolled down a little ramp at the back of the machine. The grape landed in an attached bowl of sticky strawberry juice. It didn't look very good to eat, but it didn't look harmful, either. In fact, it looked a little pink. "Sweet," said Jo Jo.

The Razin' had been rehydrated, juiced up by the natural sweetness of strawberries Jo Jo had tossed into Jarek's machine.

"If only we had some chocolate and vanilla ice cream, we could have a Neapolitan sundae, with a grape on top!" said Jo Jo.

"Gross," said Jarek.

"Excellent work, Jo Jo," the Magic Pickle said. "Only something sweet could possibly counteract the power of the sour. Lu Lu's strawberries were the perfect solution."

"Yeah, I thought of it when we saw a

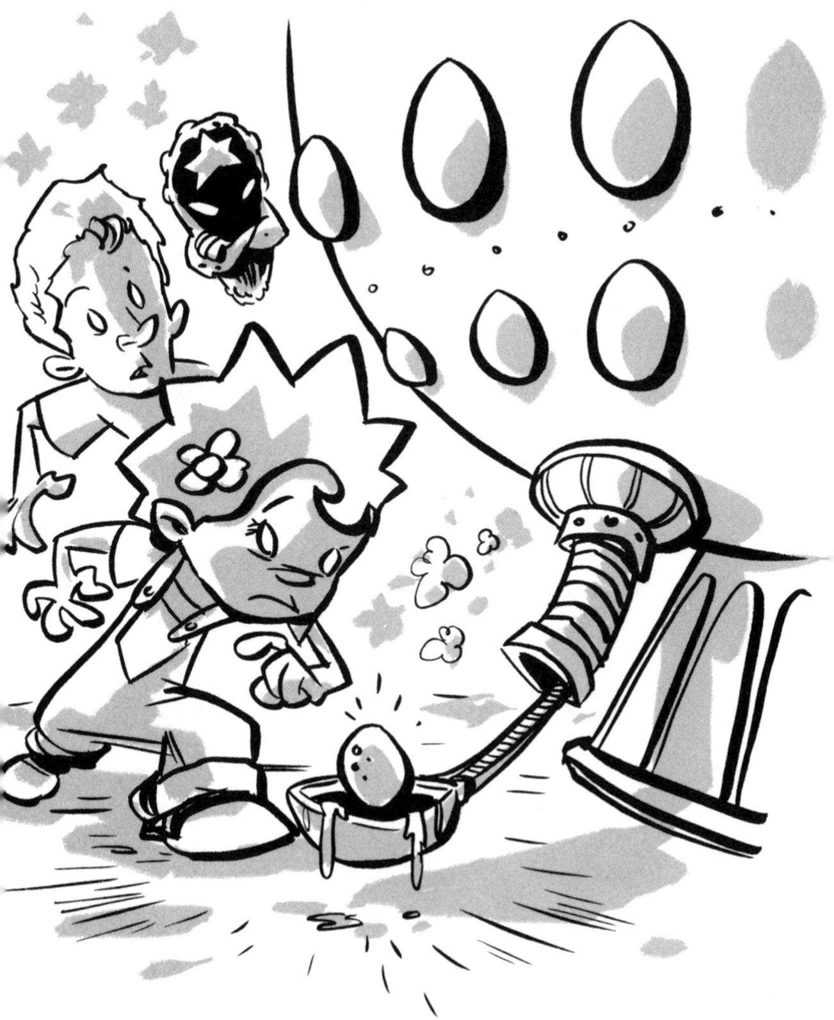

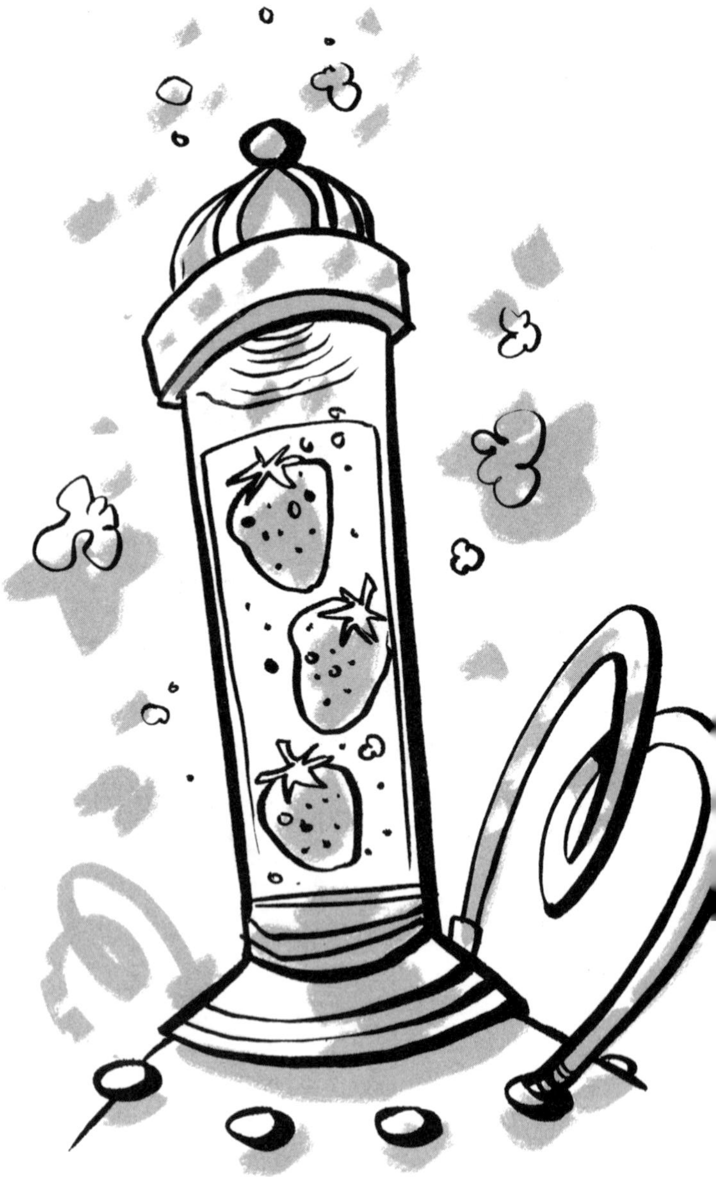

strawberry turn Mikey back into a goofball!" said Jo Jo.

"The sweet strawberry juice goes good with the sour grapes," added Jarek.

"You got that right," said Jo Jo and slapped him a high five.

"Well, then," said the Magic Pickle, "let's go release your classmates from their sour plight."

"Say what?" said Jarek.

"He means we have some strawberry super soaking to do!" answered Jo Jo. "Let's start with Ellen. I can't wait to spray ol' Lu Lu . . . or should I?"

Chapter 14

"I figured the strawberry juice would counteract The Razin' and help cure everyone of their grapeyness, but I never figured it'd be sweet enough to make people forget what happened, too!" Jo Jo said.

"It's amazing what a natural sugary shower will do for a person," said the Magic Pickle. He hovered near his computer screen.

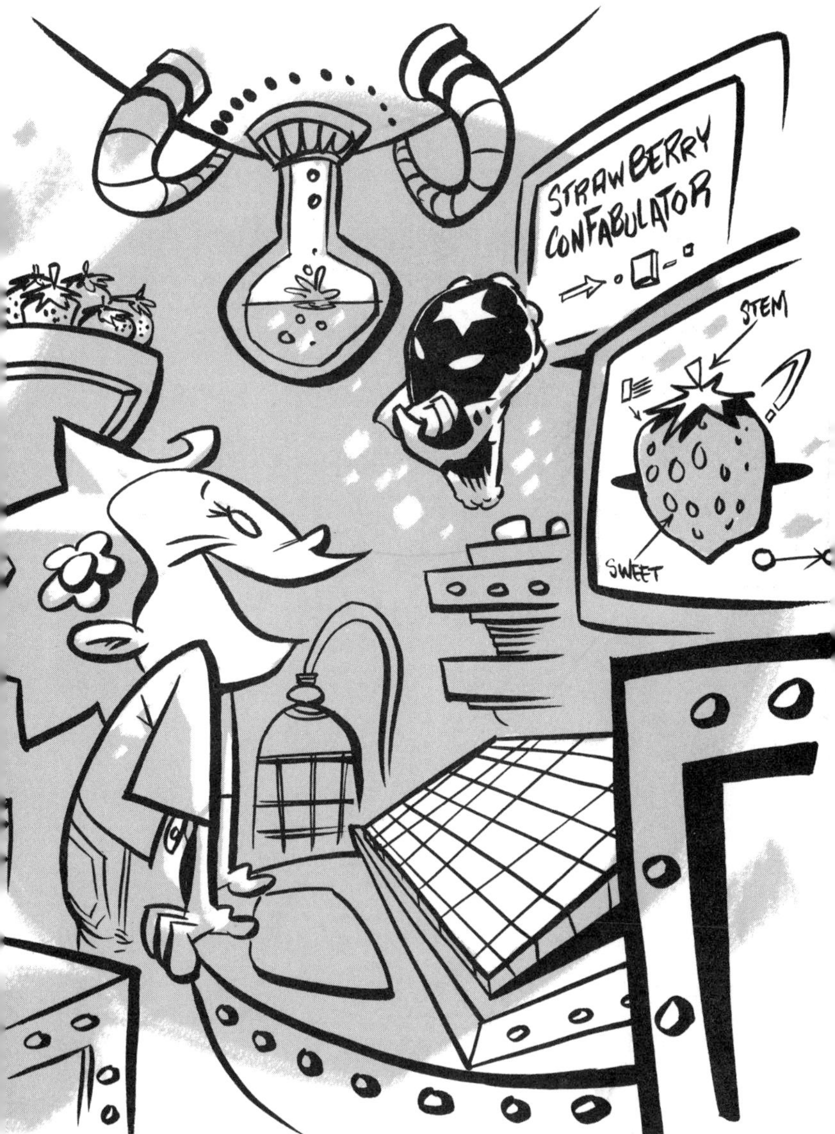
STRAWBERRY CONFABULATOR
STEM
SWEET

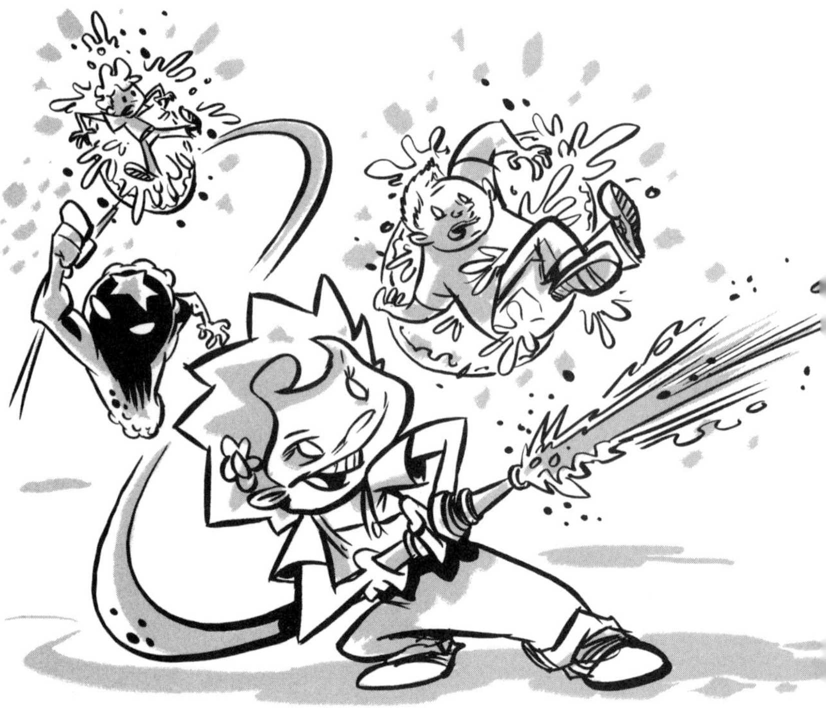

Jo Jo and the Magic Pickle were safely home inside Capital Dill. They'd successfully doused everyone at school with the sweet strawberry juice—even Lu Lu—turning them all back into people . . . except for Binky Alawicious, who remained a hamster.

Instead of a birthday cake, he got a big glass of strawberry juice.

Jo Jo stood behind the Magic Pickle as they looked up at the wall of screens. "I'm pleased we can raze The Razin' from the roster of rogues," said the Magic Pickle.

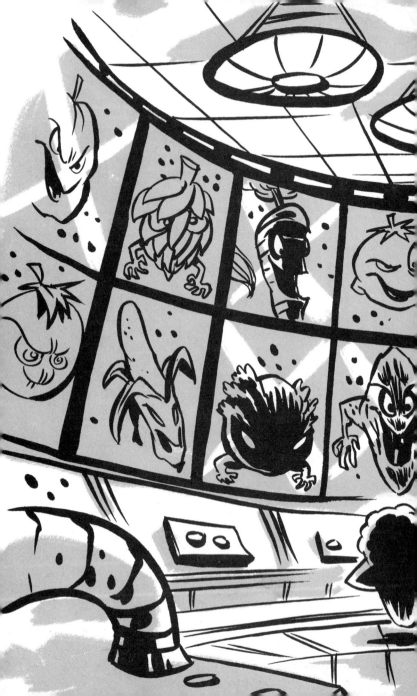

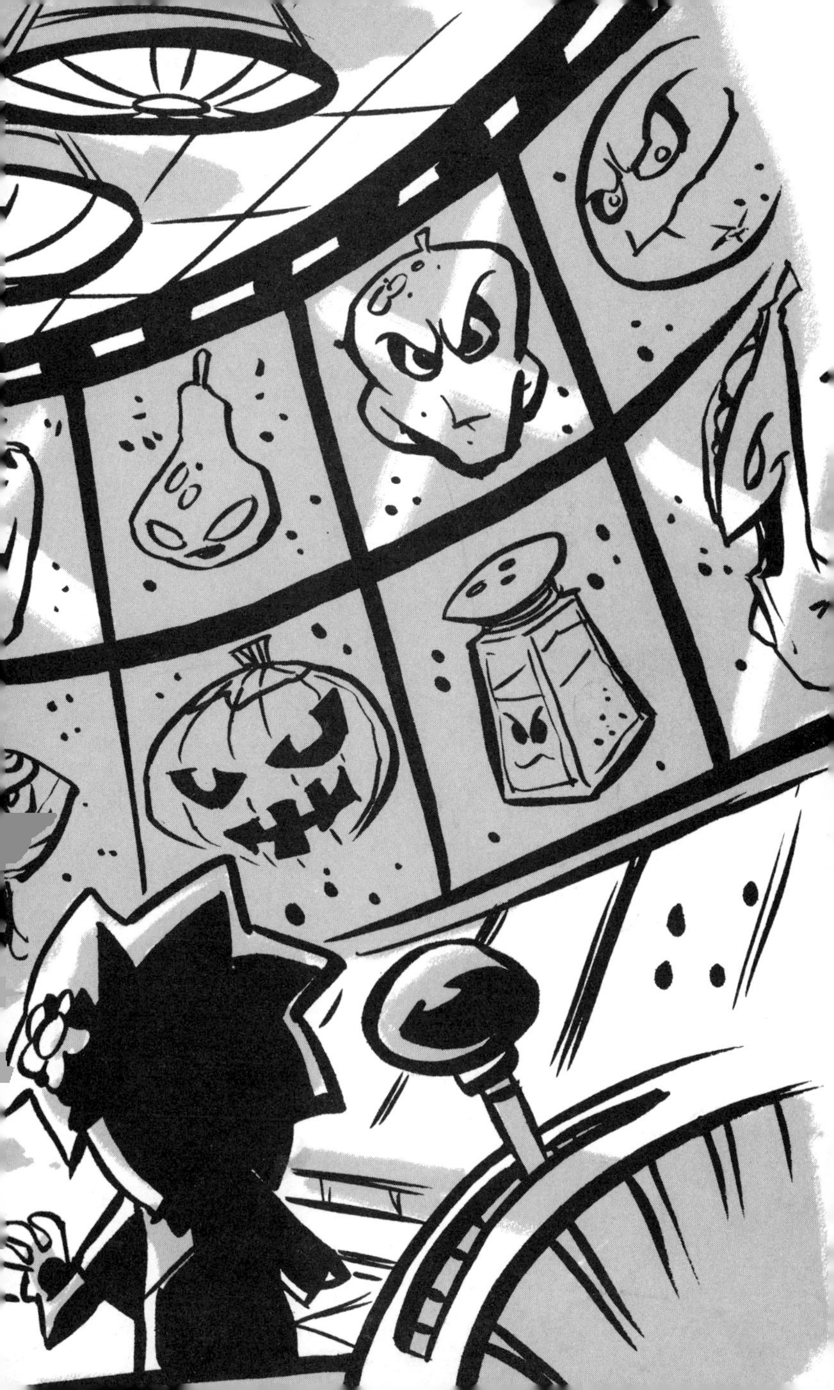

"Yeah, e'raze' him already!" said Jo Jo. Her nose wrinkled up at the thought of the creepy vine-ripened villain.

Jo Jo watched as the Magic Pickle began to type on his keyboard. A new computer screen hummed to life, and the face of THE RAZIN' appeared.

"You know, I couldn't have done it without you, or your friend Jarek," said the Magic Pickle. "It's a shame I can't shake the boy's hand."

"Lucky for you I was able to slip Jarek a juice box filled with an extra-special batch of strawberry juice with his afternoon snack. I'd hate for him to remember any flying pickles fighting giant grapes," Jo Jo said. "I'm pretty sure he thinks you're a figment of his imagination."

"I'm neither fig nor mint, my small female human friend," the Magic Pickle stated. "I'm one hundred percent pickle. And now

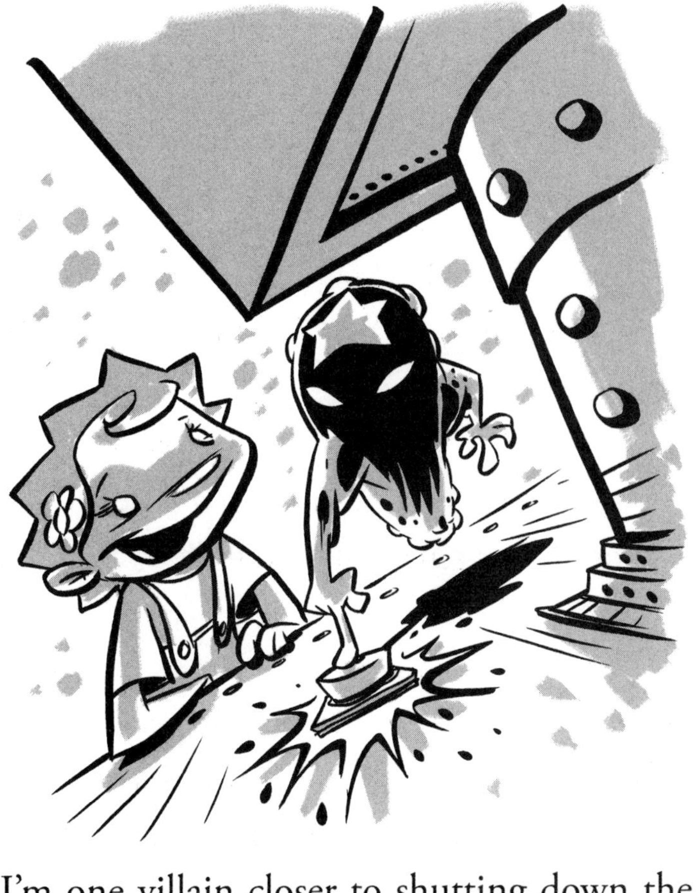

I'm one villain closer to shutting down the Brotherhood of Evil Produce."

The Magic Pickle pressed a button. A red X lit up across the face of The Razin'. They'd never have to worry about that shriveled-up weirdo again, Jo Jo was sure.

"JO JO! DINNERTIME!" her mother yelled from above.

Jo Jo ran up the steps to her bedroom. She climbed out the hatch that led into Capital Dill and turned to wave down to the Magic Pickle. He gave her a military salute. Jo Jo giggled. He always looked so darn silly when he tried to act official.

Jo Jo skipped into her kitchen and pulled a chair up to the dinner table.

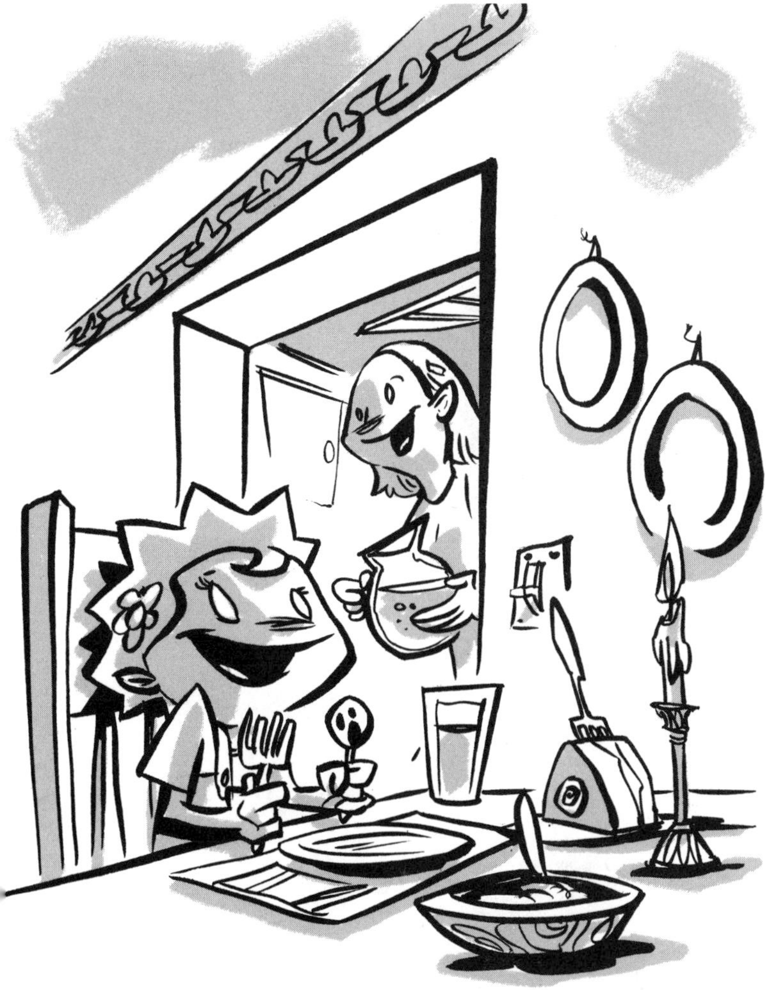

Jo Jo's mom set a glass next to her plate and said, "All we've got left to drink is grape juice. Is that okay with you?"

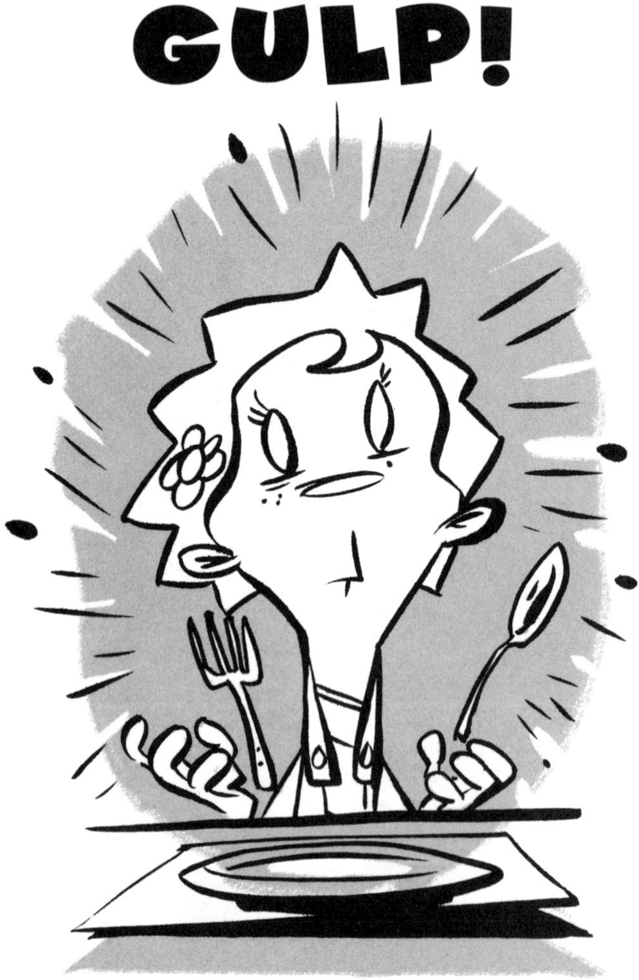
GULP!

The End

MORE PICKLE POWER FROM SCHOLASTIC

There's a rotten egg in town who's out to poach a wild kiwi but in the process creates havoc at the zoo. Magic Pickle and Jo Jo are on it!

A graphix Chapter Book

SCOTT MORSE
Magic Pickle
VS. THE EGG POACHER
SCHOLASTIC

SCOTT MORSE

Magic Pickle

THE ORIGINAL GRAPHIC NOVEL!

SCHOLASTIC

Available
May 2008

Here it is: the original **graphic novel** in full color!
Read the whole story behind the world's greenest,
bumpiest, briniest superhero, the Magic Pickle,
and his feisty sidekick, Jo Jo Wigman!

A thrilling, action-packed story
that starts in a secret lab and ends
in a food fight!

An Imprint of

Meet Scott Morse

If you read Scholastic's *Goosebumps Graphix: Creepy Creatures*, you saw Scott's super-cool art in *The Abominable Snowman of Pasadena* story (and if you haven't read it, check it out!).

Scott is the award-winning author of more than ten graphic novels for children and adults, including *Soulwind*; *The Barefoot Serpent*; and *Southpaw*. He's also worked in animation for Universal, Hanna Barbera, Cartoon Network, Disney, Nickelodeon, and Pixar. Scott lives with his loving family in Northern California.

And sometimes – if there are any in the fridge – he even eats pickles.